W9-BJL-148

Golden Handcuffs Review

Golden Handcuffs Review Publications
Seattle, Washington

Golden Handcuffs Review Publications

☆

Editor

Lou Rowan

Contributing Editors

Andrea Augé
Nancy Gaffield
Peter Hughes
Stacey Levine
Rick Moody
Toby Olson
Jerome Rothenberg
Scott Thurston
Carol Watts

LAYOUT MANAGEMENT BY PURE ENERGY PUBLISHING, SEATTLE
PUREENERGYPUB.WORDPRESS.COM

Libraries: *this is Volume II, #28.*

Information about subscriptions, donations, advertising at:
www.goldenhandcuffsreview.com

Or write to: Editor, Golden Handcuffs Review Publications
1825 NE 58th Street, Seattle, WA 98105-2440

In Memory

George Economou

Kevin Killian

Contents

3 Poems

☆

Rae Armantrout

SPURGE

Here the windows offer nothing
in the way of temporary death,

no metaphors
for old age
to be followed soon enough

by youth.
No secret formula.
Here everything is patent.

If there's a lesson,
it's to do
with eternity's hodgepodge

and the limits
of thought.
Who would think up

the muscular tongues
of the what's-it,
fuzzy and gray-green

next to the rattling
vertebrae
of fronds,

or that euphorbia
(good form?),

formerly known
as spurge.

BLOTCH

1

"I am a bunny,"
and you are not

is what I meant.

That's how it all started.

("Not" felt something
slip
and was frightened.)

2

Oh lord,
may I turn all this
to my pleasure:

stiff leaf tumbling
end to end
in slow motion;

moving blotches
of shadow

that cover,
uncover

bright pebbles

SOME THINGS

"Nee Nee" and "Ah Ah,"

you'd heard the word before

and there they were—
two ants,

miniscule and flustered.

You were ecstatic.

*

As if each feeling
was a message

from a god

with his or her
own interests.

*

Glacial erratics.

Tossed off the way
one says,

"When I die"

I didn't mean to fall silent.

from *Parrot Eyes Lust*

☆

Ron Silliman

First fart
        best fart?
            Desire to sneeze
                or to not sneeze

is desire nonetheless

        Fog
        in Chester County
            comes close to the ground
    One barely sees
that house up the hill
        the one that
            raised a fence
                just last week
            tall wood posts
                & a wire mesh
            just the third
        fence in
            the entire area
        in 17 years

    bones
        jug
      banjo
        & a bass

occasionally a fiddle

One guy
    whom I take
        to be psychotic
    is talking intensely
to no one in particular
    as he dances

until he
      picks up the
tall chair
on which I'd been sitting
      which he proceeds
        to lead
          in a waltz

    The sound ice makes
        rattling in a glass

    Spoon scrapes
      side of the bowl

    Sun swallowed by fog
        envelopes the woods
      soft, unfocused half light
In spite of the warm winter
      no insects as yet
My sweatshirt
    left on one chair
your scarf on the next

Harsh light of the lamp
this early in the morning

In the microwave
blackberries
burst in the oatmeal
that tart sweetness
bleeding through the bowl

Larks in parks send sparks

Dream in which
Monroe & another actress
are having an
intense conversation
Monroe
describing the other's plight
so acutely
you realize that
really
she's describing herself

The ways in which
My mother
identified with Marilyn Monroe
seem now
not the slightest bit comic

Dear Landlord
Dylan's voice
in ballads
articulates depression
in ballads
in salads
intifada

Too bright
this early
on a not yet
spring day

I rise to write
as tho that
were a continuation
of dreaming

What I remember
makes no sense

Guy I "rescued"
from drowning
pulling himself off
giant conveyor belt
was in fact
in no danger

tho he threw up on me nonetheless

Large
garbage truck
somewhere up the block

I hear
how its
cavernous bin
resonates
with broken glass

The more
I tilt this pen
perpendicular to the page
the narrower
the stroke of each letter

The grid
of the type-
written page
is not visible
i is as wide
as the w

Sad old man
        becomes a monk
out of fear
was that it?

        The lawyer my
                grandfather hired
        in an attempt
        to learn of his parents
        is given only
                the name of his birth mother
        "Mrs Nellie McMahon"
        tho no evidence exists
                that she ever was married
Mysterious stranger
        in the family tree
        I hold the point up
        & away from the page
My eyes shut
        on the edge of sleep

                Clothes dryer roars
                        that its load is done

In the dream
        the new pitcher
        is a young woman
                shorter even
                        than the shortstop
                        which in this instance
                                is me

        Waking, I
                realize
        that must have been
                Roberta Ramirez
        younger than either
                of her brothers

        but a better
          ballplayer than either

What became of her
   over the past half century?
Why dream of her now?

    Footsteps upstairs
       are of bare feet

   The world into which
      I once grew up
  has begun
       to come apart
    like some cracking façade

  Pesto with
    walnuts
  instead

    Orange corn
      in the mixed veggies
   served with a pitcher
    of mango

All about the hot sauce

    Over the river
    into Quebec

Oscar Peterson
alongside the piano
that mysteriously plays his music
to no one in particular
intersection by some overpass

A lone grape left atop the table

The gray dawn
will soon
yield to color

How old was I then?
Just 2? Maybe younger?
Who was she?
That she would put
take, put, take
the tip of my penis
or was it the whole apparatus
into her mouth?

I know that I peed
thought it a game
a delightful release

Why, all these decades later
can't I see her face?

The new neighbors
leave the lights on
all night long

I can hear the furnace
tho I don't know why

New hellebore
about to be planted

Now the dishwasher
with its mysterious rituals

New pair of gym shorts
with this high-tech no-sweat
fabric I
don't really like

Constituents vs. enjambments
A dangerous game?

     Brush the basting mix
       over the haddock
      Who's walking
       barefoot upstairs?

   I cut the newspaper
   back to five days per week

Too many blankets
curdle the dream
     I rise
          to sing this song

    but "sing" is such a technical term
       by which to characterize
          this gumbo
        slow-cooked
           of memory & grief

   Outside, fog contains the sky

     Inside, I cry
    because the make-up stings
        my eye & Emmett
     Kelly did this so much better

   Jack Gilbert, peeking through the window

I try
to decide
wch way to spell
thru

      Something in fact
        one does
       through a word

Consistency being the hobgoblin, etc

That being one of my favorite words ever
How does a goblin hob?

To hob & hob not

But I didn't wake up angry
so much as terribly sad

Loss being loss
therefore permanent

Nation X
wishes to express its regrets
at the inadvertent
& unintended
massacre
of so many
innocent women & children
of Nation Y
during the course of
its invasion
of the latter state

What in the South
they call keening

Incessant wail

Well, it troubles my sleep

Bernstein, Berrigan, Blackburn, Blaser
Many Berrigans in fact, including Sandy
street map for a city of dreams

Ink soaks into the paper

First battle, best
bottle

It rattles my sheep

Or just an aluminum can perhaps

spinning empty on the pavement
parchment
Pepsi
for a logo

The great lion of
Syntax
licks his chops

Forsythias
for
seething

We drive slowly
almost coasting
through Cortland
in search of gas

I try
to imagine Paul Blackburn
donning a Yankees cap
a little theater
for the reading
in this very town
42 years ago

"So they tell me you're a poet
What's that like?"

I walk into Starbucks
in Amherst NY

confident that I can get
a double espresso

Baked walleye
topped with a little dill

Joel speaks of a pen shop
down near City Hall
In New York

Keep the point
in firm contact
with the paper

How the fog
diffuses dawn

Maybe that word *How*
is superfluous

The necessity
of a left margin
is something
I don't think anybody
quite gets

Between tinnitus
& spring sinuses
the skull
is a swollen
ringing
bell

The sound of water
before it boils

Having eaten the banana
the taste of which
lingers

That there is not
a right
(or in this case
left)
answer

The bird can only echo
Can only describe what it sees

Dent the notebook's spine
makes in my leg

Pen tip demands
to approach the paper
almost at a right angle
Only when I shut my eyes
can I feel
in the eyeball itself
just how little

sleep I've had

Unlikely Facts

☆

Norman Fischer

Unlikely Facts

unlikely that the fact of others — what's a stopping point? — pouring
as if hurling something skyward so much so that expressing it
[outside the usual ideas that are words I could use] could be that/
not that, estuary, subplot, one's searching for an improvised image
but an image isn't improvised how could an image be improvised
an image is not invented it leaps out from there — its side — so no
it's in the dark that you find the names of things peek out to reveal
themselves a serious business of finding an image in the dark you
have to name so then you can be someone naming that it's certainly
a woman — no that's not a projection a designation a subplot to
storyline how about finding out what cruelty actually is a form of
laziness something unexamined rears up and bites you so no it
couldn't be just the way you think it is how it is how you see it how
it actually appears you call out it calls back so the name came on a
sound not an image that would be another sort of person use what
kills you too bad if you can't be desperate enough to believe enough
in this teetering world

It's Too Easy

It's too easy to believe in a world as it appears

yes poets are magic

a world to be in desire in the shape of her need she hollers o yes
       and then what who's to pay attention to it they all want of
       course their own rules

their uses reinforced if not then who could understand anyone what
       other any other

no,

catastrophic divisions underlie dark sexual sounds

where music comes from it's so moist and sexy but after it's over it's
       gone

why time appears not to be so

Not as Deep

struggling in the water not as deep as first feared maybe chest deep

it depends then on the artful boy

plunged into singing at top of his lungs

never mind the bullfighter!

never mind the boxer!

the water sparkles clear you can see through it

to a pale blue

a line

a line

then another

a pattern with appeal

in the spine then floods brain

so many sorts of women dark and light as fearsome as they are
       poised

as they are open to events

Perfectly Clear

although obscure

because then there'd be the illusion of something external

and you'll have you think something to be referred to

but there's nothing referred to

how could there be the referred to?

the words
the time
how could there be anything —
but no the sentence — is there a sentence? —
isn't that the sentence isn't external
has own logic
own curse and pride
but I'm here among others where are others now
in my little word?

Parts of Words
origin al origin in words or parts in wor ds
that's certain ly sex ual - if there are seg ments, wearing pants,
there's al ready in that
attract ion/repuls ion there can be dif ference all kinds variety
then a joke, it be comes a kind of joke if there are pants
then there's feminine masculine pushing out to the in ward re ceiving
every thing difficult when you' re in lo ve space be comes viscous
you can't even press through to where ever you think you half-
            heatedly are supposed to be
now when you're al together trap ed in your part icular seg ment
which is why I say
sexual lullaby — big
climax
big long rest
moment ary whole ness in dark ness
received by image
then press ing out all over a gain
much as though it matter ed
you want it not to end but of course
it ends you could leap into

Dread Word
you could count on it to appear just when
you wanted — well — it — where —
some small word would betray you
but who anyway

counted on anything to be there
in the next moment
even one's self
so it's calming
that there's yet something more and the
serious people speculate
about the ensuing arrangements, society, government, economics,
        etc they say
with straight face — even as in flames they're devoured by some
        invisible beast
collective among us
can it be accidental the Greeks
who thought from earth and sky
wondered and doubted whether we're really here
at all in the way we say then it appeared
everything we thought they'd said to us about it
that we discussed and believed
and were confused over
was a misconstrual
based on a mistranslation

Because of the Flames
because of the flames as they say warming the hand of the beast we
        were
our brain is made for aggression the sin of having
become alive suddenly rather than gradually
as if to hover
then gradually smudge into appearance maybe fuzzy faint
and then maybe not here or squinting
instead we appear definite in shape and color solid
here distinctly together it would seem
warm
against the flame burns up
grasses on hillside then some trees then more then
forests of trees then houses among the trees then bodies in the
        houses
torched by dancing licking flames

Too Late to Stand to One Side

drawn into it — too late to stand to one side wondering what is that —
within or outside it to say o that's there isn't that there or
didn't that happen, he, his character, that he did do that
not vague or questionable
yet there's doubt that there's anything how could there be anything if
       later not
is it at all
and everything is is
now is later not — and now and later also occur
probably at once or how could you tell something
otherwise nothing could be told if not now and later
here are tables chairs coffee cups it must be a cafe
writers write in cafes
they sip coffee
words come to them

Parts of Things

In any moment things and parts of things, bottles, cans, plates, forks
       manufactured for use
made to confirm wishes and dreams —
imagined they later appear in a time sequence maybe a life anyone
       lives in
then — so — OK — next a crash, slash and burn, there's fury in
       feeling when you stop being distracted by the many things
       that appear to be there
o dear yes then
watch out — watch in —
because of the sin of being alive suddenly
having to eat and push outward
like a worm in mud inching forward
finding what to eat in dirt
you have to live but the machines don't know —
no one does — a jumble of mechanics
then laws of how things fall
down or sometimes up
into clouds

No Time

next there's no time — someone tells a story — everyone's story all's
thinking and shouting and gesturing, someone deciding — it's ugly
how we're to be — how see this one place where we are — losing
        face getting face
the others to be extended shrink me pushing face in
so poor little eyes engulfed in flesh
I'm cowering over there by the wall pushing in
that's the way it's supposed to be according to the book
but he forgot how to read the book
got stuck in history in the opposite way
so read from the ground up
but the sky is also good
look down from a cloud

It's Dark

it's as if I'm not able to go any further into here it's dark
so yes I go in the dark but also only so far because I want to find
my way back but really I didn't go in anyway
because that's not really the space of it — in extension — but always
        on one spot
which explains a lot
really a lot
so well yes OK I guess I have to keep on
what else would anyone else have me
do how else to
be with this seeming
disaster otherwise if not that
far in here where it's dark
so as to break through to the second world from the first
but still be in the first which is where
the second still is but there can't be
two worlds can there — one must be an outlaw
if in one or two worlds to break out of you break in
or are locked in for bad behavior
where you are going to perform much bad behavior
causing many bad things to then occur
so you pound fists on cage-bars or smooth glass walls

as if there's any inside or outside it appears so
but you can't see that or anything
whatever you see's an illustration or
metaphor that hurls you forward
into your clothes you're still wearing
anticipating there's something more
a path, a development, a progression, a sequel, a plot, a point — or
        that there's
at least a plot
of earth

I'm Not
I'm not
of you - I'm
of

myself then there's later
this then that

how odd it all was
when it was is

so that there's this
as much as it ever was

even, the long past
is and was — how far

the violence to set in one
needs at least an other

to hate to be bitter
makes you strong to live

so there's this then that
to push off of so sad

that that's how love
grows how it goes

So Long for This
I worked or played or struggled
so long
for this?
or that?

what about the other people
in this place? who plays or pays

for that? time is already
hope but time is very old

so I think now I am ready
for this but need a place

to put it for now why not
here anyway here it
is placed in a spot

May, 2013

Ganymede

☆

*Anne
Tardos*

When the nomad's gonads came under scrutiny,
Ganymede's gametes were also examined

Sexting was considered as barely communicating
At least inside the chamber that was made of amber

Later the chamber was found in shambles
Resembling a daffodil-covered duck

The duck was a naïve conversationalist and something of an
        alarmist
Equanimity was the goal of all those sitting under a parasol

Rembrandt liked to gallivant around Leiden
Where Spinoza had also found enlightenment
The two may have met walking along the banks of the Rijn
In Leiden where the Rijn widens

Jupiter's moon Ganymede was discovered and so named by Galileo
just 25 years before Rembrandt painted the unwilling mythical boy

being kidnapped by Zeus, who was Jupiter, who was the eagle.

Ganymede was dragged to Mount Olympus, the heavens, to be in charge of moisture and rain and to be Zeus's lover. In Rembrandt's painting the chubby and clearly unhappy boy is seen with a long stream of urine flowing from his penis as he is carried off in the eagle's grasp.

*

When the eagle and the nomad
Came along with the boy, their gonads came along with them

They considered sexting a naïve form of conversation
barely communicating
at least inside
inside the goal
of the chamber that was also a bar

later the duck named Amber
Later when Rome came to shambles
resembling a parasol
Resembling a bar
Daffodil-covered duck was
Covered duck the earth
Duck the duck the
Duck was made of
Naive conversation and discovered
Conversing
and discovered by
Something of urine just as an eagle, a beaver, and a beagle
walked into a bar.

The bar was not very far.

As far as the eye could see there was matter. Stuff.
Incapsulated in this matter, life found itself to exist.

Inflating existence to the sum total of reality.

Or why should there be something instead of nothing?

Or are we what we choose ourselves to be?

Glosa Riffs on Meltzer, Mac Low, Loewinsohn

☆

Stephen Bett

David Meltzer: Gone Beater

When I was a Poet
Everything was a Revelation
no detail less than Cosmic

When I was a Poet

When I was a Poet—David Meltzer *(with nods to D.M., Abbie Hoffman,*
Ginsberg, Sanders, et al)

When I was a Poet
on a reverse Abbie H steal at City Lights
an agitprop book installation w/out much
enter or prizing, & no Peace Eyes here...

Everything was a Revelation
'cept 4 "defanged cuddly types like Maynard G

Krebs" digging your six-wing Serpent Power
fry our misspent powdered egg blues mama

no detail less than Cosmic
incl. line-out wrote for yrs truly
on ~~David's~~ *Copy,* so sweet of you
hep to head mano a mano

When I was a Poet
at young Beat poet truly yrs was a lone
T.V. Baby Dobie Gillis poet trailing
a slow beater incidentally worth bah…

Jackson Mac Low: Acrostic for an Estranged Daughter
(tailgating a five-liner glosa)
Hegemony   daughter of silence
Sentence Clovis remorse jitney Rinpoche
Reader response   perspective
Outrage won   polyp wattage
Normal cargo weight   souped-up runt

*from Twenties—*Jackson Mac Low *(no nodding… or noodling)*

Hegemony   daughter of silence
Exploding strains roll dice, this action jack impulse
And spontaneous, systematic chance-gene-
Rated sorta proto hashtag Cabaret Voltaire
Too Cagey my nightmare child, no chance here

Sentence Clovis remorse jitney Rinpoche
Icky Sam, fat l'il cloven hoof alt-right sleaze freeze
C U later die neuen Trungpa, say Budder-gater (ho ho)
Krazy wisdom alright, ein five-plug nickel
Drumpf'd off on the bubble, ich bin goodun clerk'd

Reader response   perspective
Execrable fluff'n, so who was that lit crit yokel
Adds his schtick Cowpokes & Injuns blop on est. & rad
More class'n romance, if tory'n grits, main-
Stream v. avants weren't enough already, n'est Paz?

Outrage won   polyp wattage
FFS who let the fright rite trash in?
Even odds on Xtian fascist biopsy &
Rise of the Dumpster, sick nodes in network polis
Incidentally pipped à la mort with #BackToPoesy?

Normal cargo weight   souped-up runt
(blinded by the light, it's a Hugo Ball
hat trick unter der Mac da knife
(nada nada Dada Dada
his daughter would not come home

Ron Loewinsohn: The Altitudes of Attitude

Your eyes that drive me to platitudes

Looking out the window
there's the moon.
& my typewriter

But This— Ron Loewinsohn (with nods to Spicer, EP, & SB self-referential)

Your eyes drive me to platitudes
thinking man's friend to a Braut-
igan spice, steering altitudes
out of bromide paper & gas

Looking out the window
nothing but ocean beyond us
tossed off the shoulder attitudes
switchbacks laid out were just preludes

there's the moon
oh no, not that one, disquietude
wistful as Alba's troubadour lip
(rather drive, like, a vulva valley grrl)

& my typewriter
okay, pound it out w/ aptitude
till it hurts, squeal uncle, all
the while eating himself alive

Eclogues

(Excerpt)

☆

Glenn Mott

ECLOGUE I. ERASMUS IN THE MORNING

*Across the horizon
are days . . .*

I THINK

After you, I'll give up everything.

SOMETIMES

I'll wish to talk without telling.

ADMIT

Impediment.

I BUY ANYTHING

Where nothing more is added to my name.

WONDER

Will this fit with how I get my living?

THE KNOWN

is a kind of foreground

THE ORIENTATION

to know wants to organize

IN THE UNKNOWN

is no obstruction.

TO BE

What is recognized into being.

JOSEPH PRIESTLEY

    discovered oxygen.

So the mind will recognize itself
    in thought,

and ideas, and names need not all be stored or known
    to be achieved.

We still breath in ignorance.

IT

takes a while to learn.

AND WHAT WERE YOU IF

To all other minds your solitude were a vacancy?

THE METHOD

Of releasing a carp before catching her.

THE METHOD

Of dragonflies skimming water to touch the surface.

THE METHOD

Of watching a fire cross the river.

MELTDOWNS

Over mallow bars.

STICK FIGURE HUCK

Inside the boy.

THE TAILOR

Said I'd probably have that coat for life.
And now I see, he was probably right.

.

RIVER CAMP

In a cottonwood grove. The air
full of fluff.

MY THOUGHT

Goes limping after you.

TRUTH

Doesn't know kindness, as far as I know.

THE BOY

Must outgrow his own farewells,
and not replicate them in the man.

BE YOURSELF

That you never have to remember who you are.

•

THERE

is nothing forbidding mourning.

GALA EVENT

My thoughts grow dark at these things.

It was in a room like this that poor Hattie Carroll was murdered.

SHALL WE KEEP IT LIGHT

As the skin of our benefactors?

CEPHALOMANCY

Divination by boiling a donkey's head.

SORTATION

By the Book of Changes.

ANIMAL MUMMY

As votive.

YOUR DONATED SHOES

Put a local cobbler out of business.

DAILY GRATITUDE

stinks of desperation.

ABOUT

in one's own time
over tyranny

About
in orient.

About,
in the well-join'd scheme.

THE GIMCRACK MUSEUM A PERSONALITY MAKES

In the period style.

IN READING I OFTEN ENCOUNTER A VARIATION ON THIS PHRASE

Free spirits working at a remove from the system.

ABOUTNESS

Instead of meaning.

OLD MAN RIVER

He don't
say anything.
Never did.

AREN'T WE ALL A LITTLE FAMOUS

For getting out of bed each morning,
and setting our feet on the ground.

ECLOGUE III. APRICOT ALTAR

GENIUS LOCI, S·P·Q·R

The everlasting bears no flowers. —Mandelstam

As a ruin is to scenery the essence
Not merely an aspect of presence.

In the landscape of a human absence
The world absented of this sense,

that would want pinion play of birdsong
where none was heard.

An ambiguity, in which
the presence of anyone is suspect.

So here we are. Inclined to reject
hard-hearted everything at once, and still

interrogate the shadows. Of another
self speaks a transparent one, in our place

in festive heights they soar around
the gold-flared domes, belonging

to belief in a fiction of embers.

•

DURATION'S LECTURE

It has taken years
to tell the truth
and bring it from a lie.

ECLOGUE IV. RUINS IN THE FAMILY

MADE THE PERFECT EGG

Then burnt my hand.

I AM ONLY A MAN

And need assurances.

I'M ONLY HUMAN

It pays the rent.

As to whether it is better to use "she" instead of "I" in the grievance
this is a matter of interpretation. I think each has its own insanity—

if a pronoun is unavoidable in this case.

The repulsive thought of his delicate features in old age—
when she and he entwined are drawn gaunt as Egon Schiele's pencil.

WALKING

A pilgrim's path. Not the creator of the route.

CRITICS PRAISE

In order to take their place beside it.

GENEROSITY

Is almost always prized above justice.

ECLOGUE V. MUSTARD SEED

WHAT IS TRUE

Is still true.

SHE WEEPS ALONE

For pleasure.

SHE BROODS

Over the luxury goods.

A GARDEN POT

Wherein she laid her cigarette.

THERE ARE THOSE

Who dislike anything within reach.

TO CROSS THE PACIFIC

not long satisfied with even the most perceptive observations from
    books

      a commitment to abstraction disappears

not that they don't contain some continuity

      or aren't believable

THE FOREIGNER

Finds a station awaiting his arrival.

IT HELPS

When you go, to have holdings in linear feet of manuscripts,
letters, memorabilia and other material in archives.

IT'S NOT

That observation is my only art.

A Note on *Eclogues*

Most of my adult life I've kept a daybook. There's a magpie activity about it, with its own intrinsic properties. Entries begin as notes or drawings in a reporter's notebook, or on napkins, wrappers, matchbooks, ticket stubs, receipts, or in my phone, later to be typed, printed, and put into a springback binder. I also collect and forage in the tradition of commonplace books, journals, letters, and diaries. Being difficult to categorize, these are books for which there are no literary prizes.

I have a library of such books, and as I glance at the spines on my shelves I see: Georges Braque's *Notebook*, Valery's *Littèrature*, Leopardi's *Pensieri*, Pascal's *Pensées*, the *Maximes* of La Rochefoucauld, Thoreau's twenty volume *Journal*, Camus' notebooks and those of Henry James, Douglas Crase's *Amerifil.Txt*, the aphorisms of Karl Kraus, *The Proverbs* of Solomon, folk collections of dirt farmer and Ozark wisdom; books of interviews, memoirs of artists, entertainers, and musicians, the journals of Jules Renard, and those of the Brothers Goncourt (namesake of the French *Prix Goncourt* literary prize), Joe Brainard's eternal classic *I Remember*, Paul Goodman's thought-diary *Five Years*, the diaries of Dawn Powell, and of Virginia Woolf, the letters of Emily Dickinson, Arthur Schnitzler's *Book of Sayings and Thoughts*, Amiel's *Intimate Journal*, Somerset Maugham's *The Summing Up*, Auden's *A Certain World*, and Wallace Stevens' *Adagia*, whose source was a commonplace book he called *Sur Plusieurs Beaux Sujects*. I'd also include works such as *Spring & All* with its enduring peculiarity, Whitman's *Specimen Days*, and the essays of Montaigne for stubborn resistance to categorization.

For a while, at an office I occupied in midtown Manhattan, a slip from a fortune cookie was pinned near my desk, it read: "A ship in the harbor is safe, but that is not what ships are built for." One day at lunch I found its source in *Salt In My Attic*, a 1928 treasury of adages in the New York Public Library, from which many more fortune cookies could be cribbed. A reminder to Ishmael—go sailing.

In my *Eclogues*, like Stevens in *Adagia*, I tip my hat to Erasmus, whose *Adagia* grew to over 4,000 entries and was one of the great books of the Renaissance, one that every literate person would have known about. We still accept many of Erasmus' adages without knowing their source, as in my late grandmother's favorite: "Many hands make light work;" or, "In the land of the blind, the one-eyed man is king."

The eclogue was first introduced to many of us through Virgil's *Bucolics*, where it came to represent a dialogue in pastoral settings, two shepherds engaged in light raillery, sophistry, simultaneously skewering themes of urban life and dissecting the dire sophistication of the city. Application of the term *eclogue* to the pastoral was perpetuated in Renaissance usage. For my *Eclogues*, I reach back to the original and earliest morphology, the Greek noun *ekloge*, applied to passages dealing with the harvesting of crops, drafting soldiers, affairs of state, reckoning accounts, and inscriptions on aspects of social exchange and natural phenomenon in the form of epigrams and verse. All this is at play in *Eclogues*.

For me, in the siren loud city, there is a regular practice of keeping accounts, thoughts in the cloister and in the crowd (J.S. Mill), logging-in to (Hesiod's) works and days. I'm at play in transactions without modifiers, all beginnings and middles, never ending. The epigram is an utterance simultaneously gnomic and public, and we are lucky that aphorisms, maxims, or adages never completely surrender to one era's truths or cultural understanding.

—G. M.

Fifty-Two Descriptions of Flag Burning (Part Three)

☆

Rick Moody

Florida

She was a retiree, and almost everyone was a retiree there, and at
night, when she couldn't sleep, she would walk the beach, in Fort
Lauderdale, the waterfront, compulsively steering around the young
in their careless night activities, some nights up until nearly dawn,
looking for the blue carcasses of the *Portuguese man o' war*—which
was not a jellyfish, she remembered from her time as a middle school
educator, but some kind of symbiotic amalgamation composed of
innumerable microscopic hydrozoans that liked to stun, arrest, and
then constrictively push other life forms up into their gullets. The
man o' war was like the pastel blue favored in design in the greater
south Florida area; that is, the blue wasn't of the night, of the pitiless
expanses of vacuum out beyond our hunk of rock. The blue wasn't
of the deeper ocean, of the Winslow Homer variety, the blue was
like class dynamics of a merciless Caribbean region with all its
post-colonial menace and hallucinatory pestilences, in the time of
perpetual Caribbean unrest. The man o' war symbiants washed up
onto the shore in dozens, this she knew from sleeplessness, from
beachfront Fort Lauderdale, in a line down the beach, from where

the high tide tumbled up on the lip of the sidewalk, the benches of
retirees. There was always a person with borderline personality
disorder, or similar, wailing along the beachfront that he had been
stung by a stray tentacle; his howling reverberating up and down
the beach in a delirium of night heat, and she could not tell it from
the category five isolation of being older. Was she, this compulsive
beach walker, like the man o' war herself, or like the sound of
wailing? Her children grown and inadvertently neglectful, her husband
somewhat incoherent, her time her own, behaving as the ocean
currents behaved? She had once been so many other things besides
a pedestrian of the beachfront. She had protested against the war,
whichever war it was, and against sexism and inequality and racism
and other issues, and now older she still smoked the weed, as she
had in the past, and occasionally swapped pills with others of her
acquaintance, and almost no one would believe her, if she just told
them, she of the bulky blouses and mild dishevelment, the ways in
the past that, for lack of a better word she *burned.* A simmering of
desire, summonable from the past, ebbed and flowed in the tides,
seethed like storms uprising. She could see a fellow across the room,
radiant and drunken, at some party, at some consciousness raising,
at some school board fundraiser of a cocktail party, and the reaching
out for him was malarial, notwithstanding his pretentious corduroy
jacket, nicotine stains on his fingers, crooked teeth; she was drawn
to him like the campers to the cook-out that spawned an act of arson;
she was arsonist of the heart, she was a lighting up of the sky, as
with defoliant or incendiary raids, the stories she told her family, the
dangerous hitchhiking, the journal of her life to which she gave so
much, only to throw the thing on a bonfire, the language of her journal
in her, inflammatory, down to the ash, and she followed the radiant
sentences, now past, the smoldering with regrets, with desire, and
bad choices, and more desire, and then the getting older. She burned
a flag the first time in the state of Alabama in 1966 because she
could, at night, by a willow, near a creek full of swamp moccasins,
with a couple of girlfriends, everybody so potted with idealism that
the night was everclear, in a becoming of change, and no one would
expect it of her now, she like the blue sea creature with the fatal
bite that washed up in Fort Lauderdale and didn't belong, awaiting,
desiring and aching and burning in the having lost, in this a society of

engulfment. All of her old friends were back in Michigan. It was easy to be this alone.

Illinois

At the B'hai Temple

of Evanston,

all of the candles

were replaced

with burning flags,

but by whom?

All the nations are one.

Louisiana

At the infamous maximum security penitentiary of Louisiana, there was a tradition of work songs, and the notable collector of folk materials, Angus McInerney, traveled to Angola to record works songs there. This was during the folk revival of the 1960s. Many of these songs in the so-called McInerney Cache (at Ohio State) were not written down in any way, but were rather improvised and forgotten as soon as finished. A tradition of the work song as practiced there involved rotating lead singing, as in the shape-note singing tradition, where one convict would sing for a number of verses, sometimes ten or twelve, and then with a nod turn the lead over to another. As the singers changed, rhythms and subject matter could be altered significantly, although a pulse was usually relatively constant, written in the blows of a pick-axe, as these were driven by the productivity-related needs of the convicts. Similar themes emerged over time, many of them work-related and often full of humor and sorrow. In general, there is a tendency among the Angola work songs to avoid direct social or political commentary, except allegorically, though some contend that this is a result of McInerney's own rhetorical and political prejudices, and do not reflect the songs in themselves. The narrator saw what he was intent upon seeing.

And yet among the songs recorded by McInerney is one on reel to reel XIV: II: 3 is "Burn That Flag, Miss Virginia," in which the lead for the song on June 8, 1963, is given, as is frequently the case, as *anonymous*. Naturally, as with all such things, there is disagreement about whether the song is actually called "Burn That Flag," especially in view of the fact that numerous commentators refer to it as "Wave That Flag, Miss Virginia." Presumably close listening to the finished result would support one or the other interpretation, excepting that McInerney used a low fidelity microphone in the June 1963 recordings. In the humid conditions his microphones may have malfunctioned. The words are hard to hear. That has not stopped many transcribers from attempting to get down the words, though we should emphasize that any lyric attributed to Angola prisoners in which they have not had an opportunity to confirm or deny, amounts to a displacement and a kind of aestheticized *control* of the work song, an appropriation, an aestheticizing of material spontaneously generated, which instantly makes the lyric in McInerney's rendering other than itself, and the site of dispute:

> Burn that Flag, Miss Virginia
> Yes indeed and don't you please
> I'm gonna have them flapjacks ready
> Some with syrup, some with cheese!
>
> Burn that Flag, Miss Virginia
> God almighty says so, too
> Comes on down from burning bushes
> Wears the devil's red, white & blue
>
> Burn that flag, Miss Virginia
> Light it up and flee the scene
> Feds will catch you, bring you homeward
> Saddest place you ever been

Burn that flag, Miss Virginia
The Choctaw lived here way back when
And if you say you ever seen one
The judge will give you an extra ten.

Whether it is McInerney's own work is unresolved. There are commentators in superabundance who note that not a single inmate at Anglola can confirm having been on a work crew that sang such a song, either as "Wave That Flag," or "Burn That Flag," and one critic, in *American Speech* (Burns, 1999), has observed that the dialect McInerney records is neither Black Vernacular Dialect as understood according to its graceful and euphonious rules of expression, nor a related Louisianan dialect associated with Angola, and having a mild Cajun flavor, used often by inmates of European descent. Given the imprecise rendering of the words, one can only assume that McInerney either *believed* he was rendering the text, or *dreamed* he was rendering the text, or was so driven by the desire to collect the Angolan work songs that he was willing to commit infelicities and acts of editorial intervention in a desire to capture what he believed was a pure songcraft, which was more likely a kind of subconscious malevolence.It may be relevant to this analysis to discuss McInerney's later attempt to sue the Smithsonian Folkways label for copyright infringement in the case of their release of *Louisiana Work Songs and Other Music of Protest* (1968), and other recordings. McInerney's claims are of dubious legal merit, and were found so by the courts, the actions being dismissed on multiple legal fronts. McInerney's subsequent efforts to found a small music publishing company likewise did not succeed, and as Burns noted in a footnote in *American Speech*, it appears that he later moved north, and sold insurance in Springfield, MA, where according to state records he did have a vanity license plate, MS VA.

Royalties for XIV: II: 3 have been collected in escrow awaiting a claimant with a strong case. In the meantime the author of the song remains anonymous.

Maine

How his love came to inhabit Petit Manan Island, an island in which
in summer there were no animals of the human variety, owing to the
breeding of sea birds and seals, is the subject of these lines—

In her pursuit of silence, as she put it, she had allowed her
circumstances to narrow. She came to be paid to do the handiwork
at the lighthouse and at the Coast Guard station, especially in winter,
and in the course of this to raise and lower the American flag, there,
some days, it flapped away out front, mostly unregarded, the more so
when the storms blew in;

all spruce and fir, mossy shoals, bluffs rocky and severe, and when
the winds from the Northeast arose the trees seemed to bow down
to these, in awe at the scale of inclemency. She knew and loved the
drizzle, and the gales, and the unforgiving and wet winters, and the
high seas, and the isolation, and the putting on of the foul weather
gear, and the buzzing out to the island in a launch, with her lunchbox
and a few supplies, a toolbox, for when the Coast Guard abandoned
the spot, and things fell into disrepair.

That her silence was related to bad luck and circumstances of
childhood, to which she alluded, did not cause in him a diminishment
of loyalty, on the contrary. He had himself worked as forest ranger
at Petit Manan Wildlife Sanctuary, which was how they met, until he
left of the job for, he thought, a lack of talent, in the area of public
relations. Just no good with the politeness thing of it all.

Not long after briefly sharing a ride to the mainland, an overlap in the
matter of launches, there was the encounter that took place at the
bible study in Steuben, a Wednesday. The Baptist meeting house is
on Route One by the auto repair, just up the road from the cemetery.
The preacher and his wife served grilled cheese and soup afterward
for the faithful, each and every Wednesday.

She came over from the island to lead the classes, now and again. It
was far enough to be quite dangerous in bad weather. One wrong turn
and off to Nova Scotia. Or worse. But she came, and she led the bible

study, and then she went back to her mainland shack up the road, no running water.

Oh, and the day they met at bible study, Matthew 22: "Render unto Caesar the things that are Caesar's." Does it mean, as some have supposed, that there is no quarreling with earthly authority? Or does it mean that the kingdom of heaven, which precedes and succeeds, has no position on the petty concerns?

For some months after this first meeting, the coincidental one, they took great pleasure in seeing each other at bible study. He was not sure, having never told her that there was a feeling, and that feeling was a hybrid of the candy shop, the roar of the baseball stadium, the fish on the hook, and the singing on Christmas carols, a feeling of *all* these enthusiasms, and the onrushing of spirit,

though this was the hyperbole that he felt within himself, that she knew, notwithstanding the enveloping warmth of seeing her in Steuben on Wednesdays, the flurry of awkwardnesses, and when she brought the launch into Dyer Bay, and tied up at the town dock, and went for supplies. He always tidied himself to see her. He was not sure she knew. No, he was sure she didn't quite know, because the question was of what knowledge was, a felicity or an infelicity, and what was the value of her knowing . . .

It was said that in the midst of her duties raising and lowering the flag on Petit Manan Island, specifically at the Coast Guard station, that she found occasion to burn an American flag on Petit Manan. Out of the blue she did this, with no clear motive, unless a religious motive, nor did she later indicate one, when it came that she was prosecuted for vandalism and was relieved of her duties.

And he wondered if it was just the solitude that did this to a person, or if it were an accurate and faithful interpretation of the idea you ought to *render unto Caesar.*

On the foggy days you could sit down by the town dock all afternoon and watch the boats come lazily in, the rusty, corroded lobster craft and sometimes the sailing vessels, and the kayaks, and the rowboats, and the launches from all the various island, tosspots for getting across a glassy inlet, most days, the boats materialized in the fog as though they were from the past itself, especially the past in which he had had the feeling, and the warmth of it, and the not-telling. After the conviction, she never once attended bible study again.

And then these ships passed by, and on every one of these days he expected to see her, in her launch, coming home again.

Minnesota

Excised from this text, after a complaint by the United States Department of Justice, is a rendering in Helvetica of an American flag, by software engineer Marina Lee, of Edina, Minnesota, in which the flag is easily detachable from a cardboard, or construction paper, or ordinary A4 letter paper, by you, your loved ones, your enemies, or anyone else who should happen upon the stencil, for any purpose. To reiterate, this is a flag of the United States of America produced in a copyright free context, according to the principles of the well known philosophical investigation, "The Work of Art In the Age of Mechanical Reproduction," by W. Benjamin, which flag can be produced, defiled, or honored, in any form according to the needs of the owner of the template. Marina Lee produced the original, and then quickly photocopied the original and discarded it (in favor of the copies), at the University of Minnesota, as a final project for a class whose title has been forgotten.

Marina Lee entered the University of Minnesota intending to study medicine, but, over the course of her four years, became disillusioned, in part because of a romantic relationship, termination thereof, with a fellow student of cognitive neuroscience (the duration was two years, three months, and eleven days), name omitted. Lee then began taking courses in the department of philosophy in particular and also the liberal arts in general, culminating in her new major of *American Studies*, in the course of which she encountered Benjamin's essay, while studying writings of the European continent. Obsessed with the idea that her life in the United States of America made a mockery of what her parents and grandparents had sacrificed for, she began, according to the essay that was produced alongside the flag template, to express feelings of revulsion toward the flag, this coinciding with behavior that Lee herself referred to as contrary to professional advancement, namely dysthymia including refraining from food. The flag template, copied for each of the students in her seminar, was posted online by one her classmates under the title "items for defacement," and by virtue of being posted on mostly unknown *dark web* kinds of sites, the template, though generally considered somewhat facetious as an example of direct action, took off, and was attached to many posts, particularly posts that were sharply critical of the status quo.

Soon there began to appear online a variety of graphically defaced flags, flags with flames on them, hand drawn onto them, raising an issue that Lee had raised herself in her essay, namely whether a drawing of a flag burning constituted the same thing as an "actual" burning flag. Was the mimesis of the artifact the primary means through which we might evaluate whether the flag was "actual" or not; for example, would a photograph of a burning flag be more offensive, even if heavily doctored or photoshopped, than a drawing of the flag, and what of a written account, and, furthermore, what constituted patriotism in the matter of flag burning, was it a conclusion of necessity that flag burning was contrary to patriotism, not an activity of utmost reverence with respect to one's nationality? On bulletin boards, the young and those with a lot of time on their hands began drawing flames onto many of the Marina Lee flags, often appending discussions of why they had, for example, chosen flames in blue, or magenta, and where, exactly, they procured the pigment for their stylized conflagrations. This went on, for a while, mostly without the participation of Lee herself, who was availing herself of university health services, deeply worried that to graduate without any idea of how or where she was going to apply herself professionally was going to mean that she would have to move back in with her parents and their occasionally unyielding ideas of professional progress.

The sculpture department at the university had just begun employing a 3D printer, and allowing students to use it, these printing assignments that took hours upon hours, and there were any number of arguments and disputations among the students about who got to print when. It was only a matter of time, as you can imagine, before some of Marina Lee's classmates decided to attempt to make a Lee flag template, aflame, in three dimensions, suitable for use as a plastic trinket or decoration for your holiday tree. Printing the burning flag in 3D, did become inevitable, as one student finally told Lee, who promptly interviewed her classmate, transcribed, and included the dialogue in her term paper. This flag can be used for any purpose, especially in light of the fact that you have now purchased this flag, and are a private owner thereof, including the provenance or history of ownership. It could be printed for use as a placemat, or doormat, or small carpet, or on toilet tissue if needed. It is, in fact, an American flag that can be used for any purpose, and which even violates the taxonomical commonplaces that we associate with a *flag,* the first a most important of which is *waviness.* A flag is not a flag if it does not have a *waving* essence, and thus this is a flag and a not-flag, burning and not-burning according to analogical usage.

Marina Lee repudiated the creation of the burning flag template, likewise the three-dimensional burning flag template, and, after a time, did in fact return to the study of medicine, in particular she earned a degree in psychiatry, and while feeling that her studies in the humanities made her a better doctor, she didn't pursue them any further than in her *undergraduate times.* On a sub-reddit concerning the Marina Lee burning flag discussion, Lee is thought to have written the lines: *the proliferation of these images is like the preservation of the caterpillar at the expense of the butterfly.*

Two excerpts from
Where Is Mice?

☆

Stacey Levine

Where is Mice? is a novel about a neighborhood party in Miami during the Cold War era, its variegated characters observed through the eyes of a bashful houseguest.

1.

At the dead-center of the party, I dodged into the patio's garden of palms, watching as the would-be beatnik and the poet silently unpacked boxes of record albums, stacking these on a driftwood bench while sending an overabundance of soft, polite "pleases" and "thank yous" to one another. After this, the beatnik set a disc on the hi-fi. The sound's quality was thin and tinny.

What was it I wanted so long ago, watching neighbors so incessantly?

The widow Cissy approached the clean-shaven beatnik. "Larry this record you're playing… hate to tell you it sounds like a meandering mess. What is it?"

The album's cardboard sleeve lay flat with its color photos of the musicians. "The Jazz Messengers," he answered hotly. "And by the way they swing."

"Who?" the woman laughed jinglingly. "They do *what*? Oh little Larry Smolt. Play some nice music for us tonight. A waltz."

The beatnik sighed. "How are you Mrs. Lax?"

"I've a sore hip," she told him flirtatiously. "Neuralgia. The doctor said so."

"Too bad." The beatnik stacked the '45s at the end of the bench, at a distance from the full-sized albums.

Then the music changed tempo—running, not walking.

"I've help with my pain," Cissy's large gray eyes glowed at the beatnik. "I've a special medicine!"

"That's nice." The busy beatnik organized a small subset of albums and '45s, possibly the ones he planned to play next.

"It's a nerve brightener."

"Whatever you say Mrs. Lax."

"Oh it kills pain like nothing else. I take it every morning with my coffee!" She set her fingertips' pads together, still smiling. "Larry. I've known you ever since you were a baby in diapers."

He looked around. "So?"

"Tell me. Have you ever gotten hepped up?"

"I really don't know what you're talking about Mrs. Lax."

She pointed a teasing finger. "You know all those bohemian people from the city don't you? Are you one of them?"

"I've gotta set up here Mrs.—" He gestured to the records.

"What sort of *people* are they Larry? I've heard about their odd hours. Their incense and cellars. You know. Oh-and- is there promiscuity Larry?" Her smile communicated a sense of deliciousness.

He ignored it.

"And what about the yellow hot rod?"

"Hot rod?"

"Oh don't play dumb Larry. I saw that yellow car parked outside Parrotts."

"Oh. That's Goolie's car."

"So there—you can tell me things. Because I know you. Tell me more about bohemian philosophy."

Holding a record by its edges delicately, examining the label in its center, Smolt stole a quick look at the poet Kulp, who, squatting behind the hi-fi console, made faces and rocked with silent laughter.

Smolt turned back to Cissy. "What kinda pill were you talkin' about Mrs Lax?"

"I didn't say pill."

"A minute ago you said it. Some kinda pain treatment? Pills?"

"No Larry. You misheard. You're interested in pills?"

"You just mentioned pills Mrs. Lax."

"When?"

"Just *now.*"

"Well there's the tonic of course...but pills? Goodness. It was *you* who said pill."

He set the album on the bench. "*You* said pill."

The widow accused flatly, "It was *you. You* said pill just *now!*"

"I said pill a *second* ago Mrs. Lax but I was *referring* to the pills *you* mentioned originally."

"But I didn't say pill," she repeated.

A strifelike tension flared between the beatnik and the older woman.

Smolt wiped his face, looking strained; a few curious guests drew lightly closer, listening. "Look Mrs. Lax. Why would *I* say pill if *you* hadn't said it? You were talking about *your* headaches--"

"I don't have headaches!!" she exploded unpleasantly.

"*You—*"

"You *twisted* this!"

He laughed in disbelief. "*What?*"

The poet Kulp stood. "Cool it Larry. Doesn't matter."

"Of *course* it doesn't *matter.* Thank you Harry," Cissy glanced at the poet, tightening her dress-sash.

The beatnik told Kulp: "The second amplifier's dead."

"Let's settle this Larry by agreeing you misheard me," Cissy continued, and the young man raised his voice impatiently, "I did not *mishear* Mrs. Lax! *You—*"

"You do not *speak* to me in this way! I am a notary! You kids' behavior is—"

"What's going on there?" called Bianchi across the patio, serving tray in hand.

"*You* said pill and that's that," Cissy accused the beatnik.

"Look lady. Let's tell the truth. The typical puritanical American never admits to—"

"Excuse me?" Her hand flew to her neck.

"Oh Mrs. Lax I couldn't care less if you eat pills," the beatnik tossed out, turning away.

"But it's nothing like that Larry. This is a misunderstanding!" Cissy's face flared pink. "My tonic...kills the pain," she said haltingly, weakly. "That's what I told you. *Kills* it. I said *kill*! Did you think I said pill? I said kill!"

Faces damp with the receding turmoil, the older woman and young man stared at each other.

When she hurried from the patio, so did I, still watching her face and blushing lips.

2.

I heard a commotion and followed the hallway to the bathroom, where neighbors congregated.

"Get that monster out a' th'tub," came Bianchi's voice from within the crowd. I tried to see in.

"Aw but Sal. He's so cute!" It was Eddleston.

"What in the world is *in* there?" said someone amid the crush of bodies.

I ducked underfoot, keeping close to the baseboard, entering the bathroom, where I squeezed against a damp wicker hamper. All eyes were on the tub, which held a few inches of water. In it, a baby alligator crawled.

"What an awful cute animal!" cried Millie, tender.

Marge handed her appetizer tray off to Sheila and pushed into the crowded room. "Oh that's just *Khru*shchev," she told them all, gesturing naturally and loosely, as if to make the creature seem more part of things.

Eddleston explained to the group: "I got him for fifty cents at th'Pet Ranch in Allapattah. He was a present for Sheila."

"I'm a cheap date," Sheila explained.

"Allapattah's all Spanish now," side-remarked Moose Riley from the hall.

"Yes. Isn't that too *awful*?" called out Millie the librarian. "The neighborhood's changed."

"Terrible trend," old man Lance reinforced.

"Hey," Bianchi warned from the hall. "First of all th'Spanish can come inta my shop any time. But this Khrushchev?" He jerked his thumb. "Get him out."

Neighbors laughed.

"Khrushchev's here cause Sheila didn't want him," Eddleston explained, happy-seeming, as ever, about everything. "So we brought him to Sal an' Marge."

"Reptiles bore me," said Sheila dryly.

Marge asked Bianchi: "What's wrong with keeping him here Sal? Let him swim awhile."

"No," exhorted the baker to his fiancee. "Out. *Now.*"

"Sal you could get fond of a 'gator," Eddleston shrugged, palms up. "Cute isn't he—Khrushchev? He eats grapes."

The alligator chafed his lime-green feet against the tub wall, trying to escape.

Moates poked through the crowd, holding a glass of juice. "Funny fellow little Khruchshev. Lotsa energy he has!" Laughter rushed around the bathroom. Marge leaned her head on Bianchi's shoulder and all watched the creature's lemonade-colored eyes resting just above the water's surface, his sides pulling in and out with breath.

Who could see what he saw?

Then Mike Remnick squeezed into the bathroom, too, holding his sleepy daughter Phyllis, stooping by the tub. With her round face, the child looked exactly like her mother Nina—just smaller and better-loved.

The child gaped at the reptile.

"There's the little guy," Remnick told his daughter gently, leaning on the tub. "See? They don't live long like we do."

"Aw look at Khrushchev's little face!" exclaimed Honey, pushing through the pack of affable guests.

"Yer nuts Honey," laughed Riley, peeking in. "That lizard'd murder you for lunch if he could."

"Keep the fingers away," the city's head librarian Florence emphasized from the back of the crowd. "It's a wild *animal.*"

Eddleston nudged blonde, tousle-haired Riley. "Hey Moose. Bet ya fifty cents Khrushchev'll be dead in a week."

The surfer grinned with crinkling eyes. "Sure. I'll bet. I might make a couple coins!"

"And where's Mrs. Alligator his wife?" chuckled Moates from

the door. "Gee maybe ol' Khrushchev doesn't have a girl—that's 'cause he's a conniving SOB and'll never change!"

Neighbors laughed yet again.

Then a stormy voice reached them from a distance down the hallway: "That beast belongs in the Serpentarium." It was The Woman Who Didn't Speak. "Somebody do what Mr. Bianchi says and get that thing out of here!"

"Oh *her*," whispered Millie in the hallway.

Another whisper came: "There's something wrong with her. Don't you think?"

Florence shushed them.

The Woman Who Didn't Speak appeared in the doorway, taking in the bathroomful of neighbors with huge, alarmed eyes. She'd been silent at the party until this moment, now hoarsing at them all with a salty-type humor on the one hand, and on the other, a disturbing, pent-up intensity, "You're right Mr. Moates. That animal right there is a *sonofabitch*."

Neighbors grew silent.

"And isn't anyone concerned about this creature's wife?" The Woman continued with an incendiary smile. "I wonder if she's still alive. Look at the sonofabitch's teeth."

No one understood her point of view, though a few tried chuckling, perhaps thinking The Woman was joking.

But what joke arrives so breathlessly, raggedly, and with pain on the face?

Marge and Sheila exchanged glances.

"Eleanor. It's just a baby 'gator," Millie said softly to The Woman. "Calm yourself."

The Woman Who Didn't Speak stared at Millie a moment, then leaned over the tubwater, addressing the reptile. "You're a chump Khrushchev. Go back into th' swamp and do what you're supposed to: Get married! Do you really think you can escape the responsibilities of marriage? So go on. Better find a lady and take care of her or you're *dead*."

As they all listened with bewildered-looking faces, The Woman leaned onto the tub, lowered her voice to mimic a man's. "Oh no-no. You're wrong Eleanor. I won't die if I don't marry my alligator lady. It's the other way around. I'll die if I *do* marry her. And so will she!"

As The Woman laughed loudly and protractedly, Phyllis burrowed her face in her father's jacket.

The alligator in the tub raised its head from the water, its curved mouth appearing to smile.

"Look! Khrushchev knows we're talking about him!" cried Millie.

Neighbors grinned weakly, beginning to back out of the bathroom, wary eyes on The Woman.

"Aw look. Little Khrushchev's just a *baby*," concluded the head librarian, a soft, wobbly sound in her throat: her heart.

Auto Body

☆

Esther Yi

M is back in Los Angeles, having flown over as soon as she learned that her sister passed away from a rare complication of an autoimmune disorder nicknamed the Sister Disease for its propensity of appearing in pairs of sisters. When M first learned about Naomi's diagnosis some years ago, concern for her sister led directly to concern for herself. But M passed every biannual checkup. In fact, the doctor declared her to be of "increasing" health, so much so that there seemed "no end" of this increase "in sight." Though M not once experienced the faintest hint of the disorder's symptoms—"dry everywhere the body should be wet," "pus where one part of the body touches another"—she saw, in Naomi's pain, the potential for her own pain. And yet, whenever it had come to Naomi's positive traits, M had seen no chance of duplication, as if each family on Earth was allotted a certain quantity of good.

M is now standing in front of her sister's old dressing table with the three angled panes of mirror. As a teenager, Naomi swore she looked different in each one: "Ugly, uglier, ugliest." Gazing at her reflection, she'd listen to her "beautiful-life cassettes," one of which featured a line, sung in Korean by a man in love, that always brought her to tears: "Your heavy luggage—you threw it all away." The seepage from the headphones made it possible for M to listen along, carefully, for the younger girl wanted to know what her sister meant by "beautiful life" and whether they could share in it together. But sisters never featured in the music.

On the table lies Naomi's phone, its screen flaring with notifications. The phone had been charging to full power on its cord by the hospital bed. M fingers her neck and wonders how she's made it thus far without getting it snapped.

She will have to sleep in this room tonight. Her old room, up in the attic, was converted during her time abroad into her father's rapidly expanding theological library. Now she has even less to do with that room, as with the others that have come after. She can't bring herself to respect their concrete occupation of space. What M believes in is not a god, but rather a room in which every wild or mundane possibility of her existence lives, shelved on the wall like books. The room encases her. But she is too much herself at all times to know how to look behind, around, or in front of her. So she cannot find this room in which she always and truly lives.

The phone rings. It's someone named "Auto Body 3." M picks up.

"Naomi," a male voice says.

"Yes."

"You sound sick."

"I just woke up."

"That reminds me." The voice pauses. "I've never seen you sleep. I wonder what you're like when you sleep, whether you go away deeply, or your eyelids flutter open without seeing anything. To watch you sleep—I hope you'll grant me that privilege one day." The voice pauses again. "You're not angry I called?"

"Why would I be angry?"

"I find it endearing when you pretend to know nothing."

"I'm not pretending. I really know nothing. You should tell me about myself."

"Visit me tomorrow. As soon as I get off work. We can sit in your car. Close the garage door. Listen to music. I can talk about you for hours. Here's one thing I'll say for now: you own the most beautiful car in the county."

"Did you buy it for me?"

"What a charming idea," the voice laughs. "How charming."

"What's the address?"

"On the corner there's a cart where you buy a plastic bag of fruit. You cross the street with the bag swinging at your side. When the weather's nice, you stretch out along the rim of the water fountain. Once, three men stood around you and stared. None of you moved. None of you said a single word. I hurt your car that afternoon. That's the address."

"You hurt my car. Seems bad for business."

"I'm not interested in business. Neither are you."

"What am I interested in?"

"You're interested in driving down the highway while knowing I did something secret to your car. You're interested in feeling as though it could fall apart into twenty pieces right underneath you. You see me once a month, but you're reminded of me every day. Sometimes you get so scared, you have no choice but to come back to see me, because only I can fix what I've broken."

"Tell me more. When I drive up to the auto shop, do you put down your tools right away? Do I whip the sunglasses off my face to see you in color? Does the grease on your hands wash off more easily after you've touched me? How many more accidents can my car and I possibly endure?"

"It's nice to hear your voice. I'm glad you're not angry. It must be from all that sleep. Is your face swollen? Keep it that way. Tomorrow I'll suck the thickness right out of it. Like a balloon."

"What's your name?"

"Let's say—Tyrannosaur."

"Why, do you have short pathetic arms?"

"I'll eat you up."

"And what's my name?"

"Naomi."

"What's my name?"

"Naomi."

"What's my name?"

M hangs up before the voice can respond.

A long strand of hair, coated in dust, lies on the dressing table. M lights a candle and burns most of the strand over the flame, liking the smell for how it disgusts her. But she takes care to preserve the end weighed down by a pearlescent shaft of oil. She sucks it, to see if sisters taste the same at the exact spot where their bodies hover between life and death.

As M lies in Naomi's bed, she thinks about the boxing hobbyist she has been seeing back in the European city where she lives. He's a severe man, three years younger than her, and she comes whenever she sits on his lap with her back facing him, and he grips her by the stomach, index fingers pressed into her navel. In those moments, she is convinced there is nothing else worth doing in the world. She and the boxer have forgettable faces. They never take pictures together. They never call each other beautiful. He has a nasal voice, thick wrists, and a love for his cat that he expresses by pushing the tiny skull between his hands, so that the creature appears to be wearing a helmet made of his fingers.

The boxer suffers from seizures that prevent him from holding down what he calls, with disdain, "a respectable job." He loves his condition. Sometimes he has a seizure in the middle of sparring. He likes this, he said, because he and his opponent are made to reckon with an invisible force that can knock them out bloodlessly, putting their fists to shame. Sometimes he has a seizure in the middle of his lovemaking with M. Here, too, the pair are made to reckon with a departure of a higher species than an orgasm. In those moments, M looks into the boxer's glassy eyes and resents him for not having taken her away with him.

M believes he has the potential to compete and get paid for it, but the boxer insists he will only ever be a hobbyist. "I don't want to become real to anyone other than me," he once said, "and fighting in order to win is one of the easiest ways to become real to anyone other than me." He refuses to be ennobled by the purposelessness of his rigorous training. Sometimes he lets down his guard, just to be hit, and this, he says, could just as easily have been the rule for winning. He's tired of everything people say. Don't they get bored and suspicious of their massive agreement? The contrarians are just the same. He pursues apathy as a form of spiritual purity. That's why he loves his seizures. He leaves and thus aborts context.

M turns in bed to face the wall. On the other side, her mother is sleeping. Her father is also on the other side, but at his church, and he will likely sleep there tonight.

The boxer has a German father and a Chinese mother, long separated, with the latter having returned years ago to her hometown of Nanjing. When the mother made one of her rare and anxious visits to see her son in the European city, he asked M to join them for dinner. The mother knew enough English to hold a conversation with M, but she spoke only in Mandarin. Of course, M didn't understand anything, but the woman expressed herself with an urgent radiance that M perceived as music. Afterwards, they took a walk through a crowded park. M felt the boxer's mother's tiny arm press up against hers with increasing force. Finally, the woman turned to look at M—they could regard each other at perfect eye level—and seemed to register profound comfort from whatever it was that she saw in or on M's face.

In bed, M often cries out "It hurts!" in Korean. For some reason, experiences of sharp and sudden pain bypass English and call into service the first language she ever learned, which was also the first language she ever lost in part. Such is the case when the boxer, upon her detailed request, twists the tip of a penknife into the mole on the side of her abdomen, just under the rib. It's not that she likens herself to Christ—she sees no possible enjoyment to derive from this—but rather that she wants to incorporate into her sexual proclivities that which fascinates her most about Christ, which is how he was lanced on the cross by a soldier's spear and how he broke open with blood, like some oversized pustule, and though this was no personal choice of his, it still happened to him, and if she were ever to bring herself to love Christ, it would be for this, for what happened to him, and not for anything he did.

Sometimes the boxer asks, "How does it feel to live inside the sweet room of my hands?" M proceeds to describe every photograph hanging on his walls. She gets the sense that these pictures are crowding in on the two of them, returning with vindictive force all the seeing that they have been subjected to. There is one in particular she likes to examine over the boxer's naked shoulder as they press their beating chests against one another: the sun, translated into a white circle, that would probably burn out her eyes in what people call real life.

The next evening, "Auto Body 3" calls again.

"I waited all day for you."

"I've been busy. My funeral is tomorrow. I'm dead."

"Don't talk in circles. Not today. None of that dumb-person talk."

"Let me mollify you with sweet reminiscence. Do you remember how we first met?"

"That's one way to put it. You met me first. For a long time I thought your car belonged to a lawyer type, successful, with strong eyebrows. Your car was so beautiful that it seemed against the laws of the universe for me to lay eyes on the person who drove it. To own a machine so beautiful—that person had to be even more beautiful. But then you stepped out of the car one day. How do I even begin to express my gratitude for your surveillance? No one's ever cared enough to watch me in secret." The voice pauses. "We've never talked this much before."

"I want us to get to know each other."

"But you've never wanted that."

"What's your name?"

"Why do you keep asking? Is this a trick?"

"People ask 'How are you' all the time. So why can't I ask for your name? Shouldn't it change as much as how you are?"

The voice chokes up with panic. "No, I'll never tell you my name. It was your first and only rule, that I should never tell you my name, and now it's impossible to separate that rule from who I am to you. I will honor it until I die. You're trained in reading names, you said, you lift their corners and see the truth underneath them. You said that the truth moves like grubs inside a corpse, slow but certain, eating away at the name. You hate names, you said, and you only gave me yours because it has nothing to do with you. Your parents plunged their hands into the Bible and pulled out a name like a fish, that's what you said. And now you've moved onto a new name that you can't reveal because one day it, too, will have nothing to do with you. Knowing your hatred for names, why would I give you mine and risk being hated by you? I can only give you fake names. But I worry that one of my fake names will turn out to be my real name, and you will sense it, even before I do, and you will hate me. Think of me as nameless. No more talking. All this talking is reminding you of words, and words remind you of names. No more long phone calls. Naomi. I have your hairpin. Naomi. Come meet me at the shop. You know exactly where to find me. That's me. Where I am. That's me."

The next morning, M wakes up before sunrise, gathers her hair into a long braid, lowers herself into a black dress, and gets into her mother's car. She drives through Koreatown in search of the auto shop. When she finds it, she parks on the curb and waits.

Two young men and an older woman emerge from the shadows of the garage and onto the lot. The sun exposes every crack in the swept gray pavement. Dressed in blue overalls, the three employees stand in a line and look out onto the street, granting M a full view of their faces. They help each other light their cigarettes and puff up at the sun, one of the men with unmistakable insolence. The garage tunnels away from their backs for seeming infinity, its dark mouth expelling car after car. A man, older and harried, remains hard at work as the others take their break. He drives a car out of the garage, parks it to one side of the lot, jumps out, and runs back into the garage, as if he has forgotten something important. He repeats this procedure of aborted departure.

The three employees stamp out their cigarettes. The non-insolent man suddenly grips his neck with both hands and turns to the other two. M thinks he might be choking. But the woman and the insolent man erupt into laughter that M can't hear through the car window. The non-insolent man shoots his hands over his head and then, with slow specificity and care, brings them down the length of his body, all the way to his feet, rippling the coarse fabric of his uniform. Only when the other two begin to imitate him does M realize that theirs is a desire not to mock, but to learn. Eventually, after some practice, the trio are able to perform the maneuvers in unison.

When M opens the car door, she realizes there is music playing in the garage. It's the latest girl-group hit from Seoul, on repeat in all the shops and restaurants in Koreatown. Not once did she hear this song back in the city where she lives. As M approaches the lot, she realizes that the non-insolent man is showing the other two how to dance to the song, and she sees in him something of the brother she'd always wanted as a child, a fun but obtuse boy who would round out the sibling-set and finally make it possible to form the family band of her dreams. Two girls, on their own, had seemed like too much of one thing.

The non-insolent man looks up. At the sight of M, he takes a step forward, then back, which the other two, still focused as they are on his body, mistakenly interpret as the next moves of the choreography. They also take a step forward, then back. The man runs a hand through his hair and leaves it on the back of his neck. The other two do the same. The three employees appear on the verge of throwing hatchets from behind their necks.

"There's smoke pouring out of my vents," M says. "Will you come over and take a look? What if something is on fire? I'm supposed to drive to the Grand Canyon tomorrow. What if I never get to see it? Please."

The non-insolent man follows M across the lot. The air at her back is hot and alive, full of suspicion. When they enter the car and shut the doors, she feels as though she could fall in love with anyone and anything like this, moving from mutual lostness in the world to proximity in a closed space. She watches from the passenger seat as the non-insolent man, in the driver's seat, tests the vents. When nothing comes out, she feigns surprise. But he's unbothered, impatient to move on from the vents. He turns to face her.

"I'm sorry to stare," he says, "but you look like someone I know."

"Who?"

"There's a girl who always drops off her car here. Sometimes we talk."

"Is she Asian?"

"Yes."

"Well, of course she is. This happens all the time. I go to the supermarket, and the cashier thinks I look like someone he knows. I go to the gym, and the weightlifter thinks I look like someone he knows. Et cetera."

The non-insolent man's eyes grow wide in embarrassment and indignation. "I swear, it's not like that. I'm not one of those people. This woman—she was Korean-American. We started talking because we have the same taste in music. We love the same groups. What we get on the radio here doesn't compare. The first time we met, this woman told me she had woken up at four in the morning to catch the newest release from her favorite group. Imagine my surprise—I had done the exact same thing. Both of us were living on Korean time, sixteen hours ahead in the future."

"I don't know anything about Korean music. And I'm not Korean."

"But it's not just the way you look. You also talk like her. The color of your voice, the way you ask questions as though they're statements of fact. That's not a Korean thing, right? That's something else entirely. That's about how you express yourself. That's about who you are deep inside."

"I would have to hear her speak in order to know," M says, suddenly filled with unaccountable sadness. "Are you in love with her?"

"Yes, I probably am." He laughs. "But you better not tell her if you are her. If you are her, could you please keep it a secret from yourself?"

M lowers her gaze to his chest, where a long tear in the fabric of his uniform lies over where his heart would be. White t-shirt peeps through. She reaches over, inserts a finger into the hole, and feels around in the emptiness. That, he says, was where his name patch used to be.

That evening, M enters the chapel of her father's church, expecting to be alone. But the stained-glass artist is standing in the chancel, gazing up at her latest work, a meter-wide rectangular panel that runs in the vertical from floor to ceiling at the head of the apse. The window dwarfs her. M wonders if the stained-glass artist looks into mirrors with the same open-mouthed astonishment, wherein the more she looks, the more she feels estranged from what's inexplicably hers. A week ago, the window flew in from Seoul on a plane for fragile deliveries. That high in the air, the window must have done the double work of being a window in Seoul and being a window in LA. Some days later, its creator got on a plane and came over as well, to oversee the installation of her work, commissioned in celebration of the tenth anniversary of M's father's church.

M and the stained-glass artist speak in Korean. M says she is a part-time cleaner at the church. The stained-glass artist says she is a minimalist hailing from a modern school of glass. In her early discussions with the minister, he declared the central theme of his work to be the dual citizenship of Korean-American believers. As Koreans in this country, they live in two worlds. As believers on a godless planet, they also live in two worlds. The minister urges his congregation, most of them immigrants like himself, to embrace this doubleness by becoming stained-glass windows: earthly vessels for divine light. Glass like hers, he said, can only be seen when light hits it, but once light does hit it, the glass can no longer be what it had been on its own. Glass like hers, he said, comes alive in the moment of alienation from itself.

The stained-glass artist examines M with a smile. "You are not a splinter stabbing my eye."

"What does that mean?" M asks.

"It means you are beautiful. Especially your skin."

"You live in Korea. You know it's the easiest part of the body to improve. They grow pitch-perfect chemicals over there."

"Beautiful skin is no different from glass. What makes glass light up from inside is a secret. But you see the full effects of the secret without finding out its contents. Glass achieves mystery through transparency. Glass lays down its cards for the other players to see, and that's when it becomes truly unknowable, impossible to defeat. The more glass reveals, the less you understand it. Mystery is not restraint or silence. Mystery is performance. Even the tiniest piece of glass possesses this contradiction. That's why I shatter glass into ugly shards and put them back together the wrong way. When you challenge exactly that which had made glass seem charming in the first place—its smoothness, its uniformity, its placid lake surface—glass intensifies and empowers itself. So it is with beautiful skin."

"I've been broken into many pieces before, usually after some kind of love crisis, but I've always made the mistake of putting myself back together the right way. I'd look down at my body afterwards, and the sight would bore me to tears."

"Visit my studio in Seoul. I will break you with my strongest scalloping tool."

The stained-glass artist says that her window was unveiled, earlier than planned, at the funeral of the minister's daughter, who died of a strange condition. The service came to an abrupt end when the minister's other daughter was supposed to deliver the eulogy. She was nowhere to be seen. This "living" daughter was reportedly found, by a very embarrassed cousin, in a parking lot some hours later, dancing alone with her eyes closed and chanting the names of three Korean women who had been very famous in the nineties for their music. The public concert—part of a pitiful tour inspired by the three women's diminishing funds—had long since ended. Funnily enough, the stained-glass artist had been a fan of those three women. As a teenager, she'd bought all their cassettes, flattening out the cover art between the pages of a dictionary to paste the girls' faces onto the wall. Each girl had a role: the sexy one, the bookish one, the cute one. Now the girls were forgotten women, aged out of the market.

The stained-glass artist gazes at the spot where the coffin had lain that afternoon. Maybe the chapel makes the worst of the sinners, the truly irredeemable ones, fall prey to the wrong sounds as a way of keeping them out, she says. If so, she can relate. The previous evening, hours before the body was rolled in, the stained-glass artist had been alone in the chapel, polishing her work with a cloth. Suddenly, the entire room exploded with electric crackling of inexplicable source. She steeled herself for an encounter with a higher being that would condemn her to the spot for sins she couldn't remember but had surely accumulated. She experienced the chapel around her no longer as the setting that would bring her work to artistic culmination, but rather as the stage of a spiritual trial she never before considered in her secular history as a person. So she got onto her knees and prayed for the first time.

This, she tells M, is what she said: "Hello? Am I speaking to God, Jesus, or the Holy Spirit? There is only one of me for three of you. I am reporting from Los Angeles, where I have installed my finest work to date in one of your houses of worship. I would like to request that you stop speaking to me in this fashion. I am scared of hearing sounds without seeing the mouth move, and of seeing a mouth move without hearing its sounds. Is this my punishment for making art without pious reasons for pious spaces? Take pity on this earthly artist. I can make a full confession. I told the minister of this church that the thirteen vertical bars of color in my window represent the twelve disciples, plus one more, colored in blood red, and this extra disciple is the churchgoer who admires from the pew. The minister liked my idea very much. He thinks I believe. But the thirteen bars mean something else to me. Between the ages of twenty and forty-four, I spent thirteen years in love. I remember the slow turn of a head, the long hair falling to cover the face, and, just like that, a year has passed. This is how I am in love. Let me make art for my own reasons, and I will happily give it up to a church, a hospital, a school, places that use love in their own ways. Why can't our ways live side by side? Who will buy my art aside from a building devoted to purposes that have nothing to do with me? People will see what they want to see. Transparency is the best keeper of secrets. So let this glass hold mine."

"The Redemptions/ Of the Moment"

☆

Marjorie Perloff

My personal favorite among George's poetry collections is the little booklet *Voluntaries*, published by Corycian Press in Iowa City in 1987 and later included in *Century Dead Center* (Left Hand Books 1997). The first of the book's seventeen short lyrics, "Wellfleet, 10:30 AM 7/6/79, from the deck:" explains the sequence's title:

> Voluntar-
> ily. I'll submit
> > to the redemptions
> of the moment.
> > My will be done
> in whatever reaches me /

These lines provide a nice spin on Keats's *negative capability*--the "capacity of being in uncertainties, mysteries, doubts, without any irritable reaching after fact and reason." Like his Romantic precursor, George takes poetry to be the antithesis of rational explanation, but his own "redemptions / of the moment" are the result of what he here calls voluntarism—the power to choose. George is, in other words, a poet who very much knows what he is about, whose quizzical ironies measure whatever is perceived and experienced, so that "My will be done." In this case (#1), the activity to be observed is that of the squabbling finches / at the feeder," viewed from the deck of the poet's summer house in Wellfleet on Cape Cod. The "strife-filled world of birds" is regarded with bemused condescension until the poet sensibly reminds himself that "who's to say / it's that much smaller than our own?" And, with his "Antennae up!" (#2), the poet is willing to have it both ways:

> Bird bath business
>
> very good
> though they also shit in it
> and drink there too.

George Economou is a poet of few illusions: "the thread of his lifeline," after all, was "spun out of the mountains of northern Peloponnesus all the way to the Rockies of the American northwest"— the rugged Montana landscape into which he was born to his Greek immigrant parents. Coming of age in New York City in the 1960s, he learned his poetic craft from the Black Mountain poets, the Objectivists, and especially from Robert Kelly, with whom he founded the magazine *Trobar*, and their mutual friends Jerome Rothenberg, David Antin, and Paul Blackburn. But perhaps because of his thorough grounding in Classic and Medieval poetry—in Chaucer, for example—Economou's poetry has an especially light and ironic touch: his sensibility is less Charles Olson's than it is that of a New York contemporary not usually associated with him—Frank O'Hara. The pizza poem for Charles Bukowski (*Voluntaries* #6) is a case in point, and so is #8, a shorty lyric prompted by the Spencer-Tracy-Katherine Hepburn film *Adam's Rib*:

> Calling your book *Eve's Rib?*
> As if getting even were possible?
> You know as well as I
> a good woman is as hard to find
> though a woman's a woman for a' that an' a' that
> even one of those
>
> stouthearted women
>
> a woman o'war.
> Just ask the woman in the street
>
> Or the one in the moon.

How absurd, this little poem suggests, to insist on simply parity between the sexes! Poets and artists have made much of Eve's various bodily charms, but her rib? How does that figure? The proverb "A good man is hard to find," the Robert Burns refrain "A man's a man for a' that," the venomous Portuguese jellyfish pack known as "man o'war"—all of these make for absurd comparisons, but the piece de resistance is "the one in the moon." For if the moon is traditionally gendered female and the face we see in the full moon is traditionally said to belong to "the man *in* the moon," then the woman in the moon would be pictured as being inside herself. How would George mansplain his way out of that one?

The sequence is full of such witty and charming short poems but its piece de resistance is the elegy George wrote in 1979 for Paul Blackburn, whose brilliant translations from the Provençal he had edited posthumously in 1978. Here is the opening of #3:

> Earlier over the first cup of coffee
> Browsing in *The Norton Anthology of Modern Poetry*
> my eye took in Paul's dates as page 1142 flipped by:
> November 24, 1926
> September 13, 1971
>
> .   He died 2 months and 11 days
> short of his 45th birthday
>   having made much poetry
>   many friends
>   and his share of mistakes.

The precision, directness, immediacy, and candour of these lines are again O'Haraesque—but the link is literal as well as figurative. Like O'Hara, Blackburn was born in 1926; like O'Hara, Blackburn died quite prematurely: he was only forty-five (to O'Hara's forty), both poets "having made," "much poetry/ many friends / and [their] share of mistakes" in burning the candle at both ends.

But what makes the numbers especially telling is that George is writing the elegy
>   coincidentally
>   2 months and 11 days
>   from my 45th birthday.
>   Our lives—
>   each one alone

> and all together—
>
> seem to make a pattern
> along whose edge we run
> putting in our bits and pieces
> until, overtaken, we become
> permanent parts of it
> > knitted up into a design
> those left along its edge keep glimpsing.

Why Paul and not me? George asks himself poignantly. Why did he have to be taken? It is the central question of elegy, and the poet knows there is no answer: the overarching pattern, the key design, is beyond human understanding: we can only "glimpse" it from the edges. Given his own origins, George turns instinctively to Greek mythology: he salutes the Three Fates—Clotho, who spins the thread of life, Lachesis, who draws it out, and Atropos, who cuts it off. One must submit to one's fate, however painful. And now the elegy concludes:

> So this Friday the 13th
> I write, make plans
> And think about the past.
> > By the force of what I
> will call some kind of grace
> when I close my eyes tonight
> > I'd still see
> the fields of seaweed at Wednesday morning's low tide
> and the luminous greens of the freshly-watered garden.

"Grace," as O'Hara put it, "to be born and live as variously as possible." From the perspective of his Wellfleet deck, the bereft poet contemplates the merger of land and sea, as the "fields of seaweed" blend with the "greens of the freshly-watered garden." Linear thinking--the list of dates, the specifying of "2 months and 11 days," the 45th birthday-- gives way to the circular design, in which each one [is] alone / and all together."

Reading this elegy for Paul Blackburn in the wake of George's own recent death has a special poignancy. "Clotho Lachesis Atropos": George accepted what he called, in his beautiful memoir of his dying father, "the gift of a condition" with a disciplined equanimity. *Ave atque vale*, dear friend, and may the Elysian Fields welcome you.

Remembering George

☆

Toby Olson

About a week before George died, I visited him where he was set up in hospice care. He was close to inarticulate then, in and out of consciousness, though his eyes were bright. He'd spoken earlier about the annoying dancers in the street below, one of the hallucinations has was having, and I was wondering if he knew who I was and why I was there. So I asked him, "Do you know where you are?" After a moment, he raised his thin arms, the pose of a flexing muscle man, then pointed over his shoulder. Then he grinned. Of course. PowerBack was the Philadelphia rehabilitation center where he spent his final days.

I met George and Rochelle when I was a graduate student at Long Island University, a new arrival, and George was kind as he welcomed me into the company of poets in New York City. I remember when he introduced himself: "Some people think I'm Hawaiian," followed by that kind, dignified smile. It was nineteen-sixty-six, George Economou in his careful Greek afro.

In the first meeting of a freshman composition course, the students eager and nervous, George stood in front of the class, then slowly opened his sport coat to reveal a foot long hunting knife in its scabbard at his hip. He wasn't smiling, but after a few awkward moments the students got the joke.

And another one. And arrogant student baseball player explained that he'd have to be late because the class interfered with practice. Three time he strode into the room fifteen minutes late, and George let him know that was the last time that would happen. On the day of the following meeting, the classroom door locked, there was a tapping. This time the student was in full baseball uniform, late again, and George opened the door to his insistence. Just one more chance. Then Professor Economou squatted down, raised his thumb like an umpire, and growled, "Yourrrre Out!"

As the years passed, there was basketball played awkwardly in the gym at LIU and football struggling through a sandy beach on Cape Cod. Once George and Rochelle had taken summer residence in their house on the Cape, there was drinks and dinners, poetry readings at the library in Wellfleet, musseling and oyster picking. On one outing, we'd gathered one hundred and fourteen legally, and I remember sharing them with the Rothenbergs and Armand Schwerner, there for a brief visit, though perhaps I confuse the past, as George did in his final days at PowerBack. And there was also Professor Economou showing me a fake comic footnote he'd included in a scholarly article. We laughed about that.

Once George told me about a dream he'd had. In it there was a popcorn machine and a beautiful, seductive young woman standing beside it. George put a coin in the slot, and a few kernels dribbled out. "Is that all you got, big boy?" the woman asked. George banged the machine with his elbow, and soon the room was flooded with popcorn up to their knees. "What do you think this dream was about?" George asked me, that twinkle and knowing smile. We both knew the answer. Our time together could be serious and intellectual, but what I remember most was comedy, kindness, and gentle laughter.

Once in the faculty lunch room at LIU, George lingering over his Cup-a- Soup that he called Cup-a- Chemicals, there were the songs of mocking birds, chickadees and mourning doves. People were looking around. How did they get into the room? Where were they? George's melodies. He could do many birds and animals. He'd brought wonder into the room.

This was the George I knew. And loved.

A Set of Funeral Dances Mourning George Economou

☆

Robert Kelly

George George Georgios
worker of the earth—
farmer? Fabulator!
Of such narratives as hold
the earth in their hands
and slowly, over ages,
give the earth back to us.

And George told.

*

Remember remember?
For us in school it is always
September. We listened
and smiled at learned jokes
and made one too.
Professor Nelson teaching Spenser.
All day I sat reading the Faerie Queene.
We smirked a little how the wise men talked,

Professor Nelson teaching Spenser,
I sat all day and read The Faerie Queene
We walked out and coffeed where we could
Professor Nelson reciting Colin Clout
and you remembered, remember?
The hall I sat in was called Philosophy
He explained the rustic, Tudor yokel, to us
to you who knew full well
how pigs eat rattlesnakes
and how far the diner is for Sunday brunch,
Professor Nelson taught us Spenser
All day I sat and watched them come and go
You imitated him sweetly, you knew the land,
the urgent earth that makes us speak
all day I watched them go and be gone.

*

In the islands they dance
at funerals, to please the land
(there is so little of it)

to please the land with music,
that makes sense, and bodies
shaped and shaken by the air

they dance to, to give the land a gift
and plead with it to take
their brother in or their lover

their mother their children in
or even now and then
a poet given back by the sea.

*

Late Middle Ages
Early Renaissance

that was your dance,
so many pages

butterflies fluttering by
over the grain fields of Montana
where the Renaissance
is still awake, the Reformation
any minute now, and one-sixth
of the whole Canadian frontier
shimmers just north of us he said,
he said and I believed him
because it's always wisest
to believe a dance. I knew
a dancer once and as I watched
I saw that dance can never lie.

*

Not Athens, Kalavrita.
The real Greece is inland
where philosophers fear to tread
and the churches dealt more
gently with the older gods,
the ones who came in male and female
and even in between,
the gods who knew about beauty
and gave it to those who
knew how to take, the dance of taking,
inland farmers who studied
the earth and listened
to what it says, farmers
no Gnostics, no Sophists,
no restless Odysseus, no pale
Alexandrian pastorals. Earth
is work. Georgios means
the one who works the earth,
who stands on the land and holds
his wife, stares the weather down
and listens to her magic spells.

Thank the gods you married well.

*

Now I must go down
and feed the crows
who teach me how to dance
to such long sluggish lines
by being quick. The child
of any this is something else--
the crow taught me that.
And explained that all we really
have to do is change our minds.

Georgic

☆

Peter Hughes

for George Economou

it's been a long time since the Georgics
George but of course it's always next season's
away fixtures sneaking through the sentence
that occupy the fleeting sunlit glimpses
disappearing at the far end of the mind's
garden centre as someone said in Rome
the orchestrated harmonies & fits
of the individual human being
seated at an outdoor café table
such as this & staring at a forged sense
of fertile serenity chamfered to
a haunted early evening's green despair
tapping my foot to your Nashvillanelle
echoing clearings in the head such as
that allotment morning in September
(24th) a plastic watering can
plunged under the surface of the brimming
waterbutt when you feel as well as hear
imagined goddess whispers up your sleeve

The Outward Journeys of George Economou

☆

Karen Emmerich

One of my favorite poems by George Economou has become even dearer to me after his death:

Day of Disembarkation

It would be odd to call them Odysseys,
being outward, not homeward, bound,

lives made over by landfalls in strange cities
in spaces of magnitudes beyond magna.

Submission to a cyclopean physician
on an island more foreign than Phaeacia,

though penultimate stop of the passage,
certified the transference of homeland

and relegated Peloponnesos or Crete
to a recessive future in memory's eye,

despite a parenthetical return to bring
a woman away, not come back to her.

The couple married America and planted
a tree that would branch and burgeon into

complexions and tongues not seen or heard before
that momentous day of disembarkation.

The poem is most obviously about George's parents,
transplants from Greece to Great Falls, Montana, where George
was raised. But it also now feels like a poem about George himself,
whose day of final disembarkation was preceded by a multitude
of outward journeys: from Montana to New York to Oklahoma
and beyond, as he entered both academic and poetic worlds.
And of course there are the outward journeys of his writings and
translations, which grow out of prior works only to branch and
burgeon with each new reader and reading, in combinations of
tongues and minds likewise never heard of before. Like many
of George's poems, this one also marks its relationship to prior
journeys, entering into implicit conversation not only with Homer but
also with C.P. Cavafy, whose work George translated so wonderfully.
Just as Cavafy's "Ithaka" recognizes the destination to be little
more than an excuse for a life full of pleasure and joy, learning and
experience, "Day of Disembarkation" rejoices in the unknown, the
unplanned, the magnitudes of experience one can only recognize
in hindsight, and perhaps never fully grasp even then. Indeed, the
poem seems to have little space for nostalgia, or for anything but
forward movement and growth—and so, in its way, it helps us grieve
a loss by insisting on the unknowable but surely very rich futures of
what is no longer here.

I met George in 2010, when I was a postdoc at Princeton.
He was a frequent presence at Hellenic Studies events, braving
interstate traffic from Philadelphia to come up for talks and readings.
I already knew of his poetry, and he had reviewed a book of my
translations—but once I got to know him, I was continually bowled
over by his boundless generosity as a reader and interlocutor.

When I moved away on my own outward journeys (only to return a few years later), we continued to talk on the phone and read one another's work, with George sending drafts and publications at a prodigious rate that was also deeply inspiring. I was just setting out on an academic career, and George's example was an important one for me. At a time when many senior colleagues were advising me to put translation aside for a while and concentrate on my "real work," George was a scholar, poet, and translator who had managed to keep all those many selves in play throughout his career, and was still flourishing well into retirement. His examples reminded me that I would find the Ithaka of post-tenure life poor indeed if I let myself atrophy on the way there, if I neglected the very things that made me set out on the journey in the first place.

And of course George's many selves were really just one self, which refused to be catalogued or compartmentalized. George's translations *were* scholarship. So, arguably, were his poems. In fact, the distinction between creative work and scholarship was one that George challenged for decades, not only as a scholar of medieval literature whose verse translation of *Piers Plowman* represents the culmination of years of scholarly engagement with the work and its texts and contexts; not only as a translator of both ancient and modern Greek texts that combine deep erudition and an equally profound understanding of what makes a poem work in English; but also as a poet whose work was, like most good writing, steeped in a practice of reading—of texts in ancient Greek and Latin, of works of medieval English literature, of twentieth-century poetry and philosophy, of modern Greek literature and history, and much more—for which I can find no more suitable word than scholarship. His *Ananios of Kleitor* (2009) masquerades as a monograph about a non-existent ancient Greek poet, containing pseudotranslations, copious footnotes and endnotes that track the supposed sources and reception of the fragments, even a fabricated correspondence between jealous scholars—whose Jack, signing "anxiously but sincerely [Yours]," can't help but remind us of Jack Spicer's letters to a long-dead Lorca whose posthumous poems he translated. And while the book is certainly, in part, a send-up of scholarly conventions, it is also deeply rooted in a knowledge of those conventions, creating a kind of playful knowledge about the field that also evinces deep respect.

When George came to visit one of my undergraduate classes in 2014, we spoke precisely about this link between humor and respect, how a sense of humor regarding your work and self is crucial to cultivating respect for others. We also spoke about the ethics of reading and interpretation, taking as our prompt a passage from *Ananios* that juggles references to Plato's *Ion* and the 11th-century Michael Psellus's mention of a courtier in Constantinople who compliments the emperor's mistress by quoting two words from the *Iliad*. This anecdote, George writes,

> reveals the cultural synergy of a distinctive literary sophistication that paraded through the cosmopolitan society in which he and his contemporaries lived. It is clearly a very late, if perhaps not the last, faint glimmer we have of a form and practice of literacy that is far removed from that of our own time and ken. For us, continuity and connection with such poetry must be made through the sweat of our brows. To engage poems as old to us as Homer's were to the Byzantines—indeed older and stranger to our eyes and ears—we must study long and hard. And we must produce leaders in the persons of scholars upon whose individual and collective efforts we are utterly dependent to recover the discourse of past generations from their rare and, at times, intractable physical embodiments, even in the smallest of pieces, artifacts that have fallen prey to the relentless pursuit of random destructive conditions.

If the poem I opened with praises the outward journey into an unknown future, this passage here praises something that seems quite different: the meticulous, insistent scholarly reconnection with the past. Yet in my experience of George and his work, these are not contradictory but complementary tendencies. For me, George Economou was a scholar, translator, and poet whose work embodied precisely the practice of literacy he claimed has died out. Just as the tree must root in order to branch in "Day of Disembarkation," so too does this sweat-of-the-brow dedication to scholarship and art and the poetry of the past allow new poetry to flourish. Together, these pieces present George's own elegy to the future. I am grateful to be moving forward by moving back to and through his words, carrying them with me on yet another outward journey.

In Memory of George Economou

☆

Rochelle Owens

No sound...no color
pleasant... no religious imagery
cultural...
O my darling
I'm getting deaf O my darling
I'm getting
deaf O my darling
I'm getting deafth O my darling
tharling listhen
to me while
I become the deafest
O my darling
you are the dearest to me
what depth it is
to become deaf O my
tharling my tharling
O my darling listen to me
while I talk
about the Frankish
Empire and the bush cranberry

and the dither
of ancient battles and who
endowed you
with beauty and why I am
wise as a penny
and shrinking in death
O my darling
I'm getting dumb O my
darling I'm getting dumb
I'm so dumb
O my darling I'm getting blind
O my darling I'm getting blind

Preminger

☆

Kevin Killian

It's a long poky drive for Jimmy Stewart and his tan convertible glides, hugging the ground, the battered ground of Michigan, while Duke Ellington's score begins its infectious, crazy sweep through your brain. It looks so crummy—and white—around there in *Anatomy of a Murder* country that at first the jazz sounds like a surrealist intervention, like the way graffiti works. (Ellington's music provides a baseline throughout, in a kaleidoscopic variety of tones that help propel *Anatomy's* bleak, melancholy scenes into the semblance of individuation; he and his band appear in a roadhouse scene where James Stewart seems to know him well. "Hiya, Pie Eye!" cries out Stewart with a weird bonhomie, and you're thinking, "Pie Eye, how racial is that?")

The taillights seem to pause for a moment as he cruises past the big sign that reads, "Welcome to Iron City," while in the distance Preminger allows a distant view of impossibly large foundry equipment, churning and smoking even at nightfall, for rust never sleeps. I've seen a movie like this before, that begins with the hero coming back to town, almost on autopilot, not really seeing his surround, he's done this drive so often before—but he's passing through an environment that fairly staggers that viewer. I guess it's a common trope in the cinema--it's the setup for the 2018 Spielberg gaming extravaganza *Ready Player One.* It's everywhere. but when done right, it can still chill and thrill you.

In the sheriff's office, Ben Gazzara as the arraigned Marine peers at the Wanted posters up on the wall and snickers. "They got the ten best-dressed dames," he cracks, "the ten top teams, the ten top tunes, and now the ten most wanted." Very wry, but verbally something's off: he's saying, "the ten top" this and that where we would say, "the top ten." Is it a regionalism, to show that in Michigan they have their own way of saying things--perhaps of considering things--and here, ten precedes top? Is it a sign of how neurotic Lieutenant Mannion is? Stewart betrays nothing but amused contempt. "That's the American dream," he counters. "Those boys made the grade."

Otto Preminger always has something going on, though *Anatomy of a Murder,* which must have seemed ultra shocking in 1959, suffers today from lack of a big twist. It's got one twist, but is that enough payoff? We argued about this, one of us crying out, is that all there is to it, and me in measured tones judging this among the most interesting movies I've seen at least since *Ready Player One.* Basically the picture pairs a couple of troubled, randy young method actors, and another young woman with secrets on top of her secrets (Kathryn Grant, then the wife of Bing Crosby). The young people are embroiled in a rape-murder scandal so big it's shaken Iron City to its foundations, and Ben Gazzara calls in a trio of graying, middle-aged professionals to help him out—James Stewart as Paul Biegler, the attorney drowning in his own indifference; his housekeeper/manager Eve Arden as Maida Rutledge; and his drunk friend, Arthur O'Connell, in the movie a father figure for Stewart even though the two actors are the same age. Stewart, Arden, O'Connell were all born within a few months of each other in 1908, and religiously abstain from the slightest sign of sexuality here, it's as if they have ceded sex to the Actors Studio. Where is the Stewart who stalked like a seething teen through the second half of *Vertigo,* or who made his binoculars into an extension of his hard-on in *Rear Window?* He's strange here, but absent from the passions that apparently animate the younger set. This leaves Gazzara and Lee Remick to act out all the sex in the picture, which they do by leading with their genitals in every scene they're in.

Remick is playing the role Lana Turner walked away from, and she acquits herself well, lounging inappropriately across any horizontal surface in a supertight serge playsuit designed for Lana, and a tiny little Peke who holds a flashlight in its teeth. Remick's vampy, trampy performance was something Lana Turner could do without thinking, and sometimes you see the wheels clicking in Remick's head about which way to thrust her hips at a certain second, whereas Turner would have just slid them there on autopilot. Now it's coming to me, the movie I was trying to recall which opens with a long sequence, under the credits, in which the oblivious lead drives a convertible through a startling, ever-changing panorama of twilight scenery and doesn't notice—it's Lee Remick herself, in Blake Edwards' later (1962) *Experiment in Terror*, which has her crossing the Bay Bridge into the most glorious and glamorous San Francisco cityscape you can imagine, but not really noticing, not even when she gets to her ideally situated bungalow on the very top of Twin Peaks—and Henry Mancini's sinuous, doom-laden love music throbs under her like a fine engine. Edwards must have been watching *Anatomy of a Murder*, must be re-staging it here.

I wonder if everybody has movies that, if you're flicking through the channels and you land on one of them, you throw away the remote, call out for pizza, and you just sit there until the movie is over. For my wife it's *Carrie*. For me, it's *Valley of the Dolls, Velvet Goldmine*, and *Exodus*. Preminger's *Exodus* must have been on TV a million times yet every time I hear Jill Haworth call out for "Kit-tay," my heart melts like a roto rooter in a chocolate milkshake. Jill Haworth, as "Karen," the displaced orphan from planet Weird, is just as talented as Jean Seberg (Preminger's previous protégée) but in the opposite direction, childish where Seberg was aggressive and cocksure, and her British accent, like something out of *Children of the Damned* with the pursed vowels, gets me every time! Playing "Karen" can't have been easy but it is a part any star would like to sink her teeth into, a Holocaust survivor yearning to find love again with Sal Mineo, and yet drawn to the mature, and equally blonde, charms of Eva Marie Saint.

Saint plays Kitty Fremont, an American nurse who's seen it all and yet feels sorry for poor little Karen, really only a little girl despite her chronological age which I never did figure out. The movie takes place during the founding of Israel in the days immediately after World War II ends. The truth is, you don't see many movies about the bond between a teen girl and a mentoring woman--well; *Carrie* is one, I suppose, and the gym teacher played by Betty Buckley has a no nonsense briskness when dealing with Sissy Spacek, PJ Soles but especially Amy Irving, in whom she sees part of her youthful self. In *Valley of the Dolls* it's Helen Lawson observing wryly Neely O'Hara's climb to the top, except that the screenwriters deleted Susann's original idea of an admiration and camaraderie between the two, and just left in the catfight parts. And in *Exodus*, the movie may be about how awful British officials are, and how Palestinians deserve no rights, but really it's all about Eva Marie Saint and what a grown woman can do to help a young girl out of a selfless altruism crossed with an Ingmar-Bergman *Persona*-esque confusion of identities, for obviously on some level "Karen" and "Kitty" are the same person at different stages of her life. Haworth speaks Kitty's name with an exaggerated and delightful tenderness, as if she can't believe a grown woman could be called after a kitten. "Kit-tay," she says (and she must say it about 150 times in the three and a half hours of the movie). A reviewer on Amazon says of *Exodus* that Kitty, excuse me, Eva Marie Saint, spoils the movie in the same way that Kim Basinger spoils any movie she's in. How unfair to both great stars, each of whom plays a character called "Kitty" in important and mind-bending films (Kim, of course, played the TV fashion reporter Kitty Porter in Robert Altman's misunderstood *Prêt-a Porter*.) And what about *Kitty Foyle* (Ginger Rogers)? Maybe "Kitty" is a blonde sort of name, like Pussy Galore in *Goldfinger*. Anyhow the scenes between Saint and Haworth, among the most affecting of all time, make me realize that what's missing from *Anatomy of a Murder* is any sort of rueful mother-daughter-like scene between Eve Arden and Lee Remick— it's almost as if Preminger is trying to frustrate the audience by not giving us what we want—a scene in which Eve Arden gently takes Lee Remick into another room, then shuts the door and slaps her face, ordering her to tone down her makeup, stop wearing jumpsuits, and leave the Peke at home for once. "I know, I know, a man feels good in your arms on a moonlight Michigan night," she would say, softening a bit. "But honey, I'm here to tell you it's gonna end with a smile for everyone but the girl."

Mother-daughter love is the backbone of Preminger's *Advise and Consent* as well, though it's well concealed under a surface patina of talky, self-important men. Too well concealed perhaps: after watching the film for half an hour on DVD my wife walked out of the room in frustration at the lack of women in the picture. Well, it's set in the Senate, a virtual boys club (though one female senator appears), but the longer I stayed on watching it, the more Preminger's film impressed me precisely because of its female energy and involvement. It's true that the bulk of the plot has men running about trying to sway an important vote, and one loses track of who's who pretty easy, though individual performances are strong. Walter Pidgeon is sedulously sharp and on top of things as the Senate Majority Leader, summoned by an ailing President to nail down his nomination of a controversial candidate for Secretary of State. Listen to me, rattling off these terms so glibly like I knew something about Senate procedures! But that's why Preminger's pictures work, you get to understand whole bodies of procedure on a mechanical basis; the procedures are dramatized so that education becomes, like eating, a matter of unconscious digestion. Preminger sends up his own mania for pedagogy in a scene early on where Gene Tierney guides a French ambassador's wife through a typical day at the Senate; they sit in the visitor's gallery and have one of those amusing, "Oh but we don't do that in France" chats. The Frenchwoman asks if the senators sit on the right or left of the chamber to denote that they are of the Right or Left, and Tierney glances at her delightedly, as if there were politics in America! Other great performances include Tierney herself, making a modest comeback after years in the mental hospital, her face left all drawn up and puckered as though treatment had sealed up her inner light. Charles Laughton is hammy, perhaps, but he disappears inside his own reprobate of a Southern reactionary, the linchpin of the opposition to the nomination. If it were just for Pidgeon, Tierney and Laughton, the movie would have had the best acting of 1962 (except for "Tippi" Hedren, who is always our master), and yet there are another dozen or more performances of nearly equal weight.

Top billed Henry Fonda, surprisingly, isn't one of them. It's odd the way Preminger must have cast Fonda for his box office value, and then given him nearly nothing to do, while lesser stars like Peter Lawford, Franchot Tone, Inga Swenson, Paul Ford and

George Grizzard get big scenes. The movie builds inexorably
not towards an issue per se, though the fuss around Leffingwell's
nomination is all about his involvement, as a young man, with
communist front organizations in the USA, but rather towards a pair
of deaths. Franchot Tone, as the brilliantly pragmatic President,
is apparently dying of cancer (in his very first scene he's shown
gobbling down a handful of pills), and another character is drawn
into suicide after blackmailers provide proof of a gay romantic affair
back during the war. Is Preminger prophesying a future with more
balanced gender divisions? Two children appear in the film, a
boy and a girl—one of each, as it were. The little girl, "Pidge," the
daughter of Don Murray and Inga Swenson, looks to be about four
or five, too young to enter in the plot in any significant way—and it's
weird her name is "Pidge," the name Hollywood pals called Walter
Pidgeon. But the boy, Henry Fonda's stalwart son, is played by
Eddie Hodges with his customary Novocain-face deadness—Hodges
was once a big box office draw, though it's hard to see why at this
date—he honestly looks petrified at appearing on camera. In the
scene where he hears his father arguing with Don Murray, he's
hiding behind the door and his direction must have been, "Think of
nothing." A few years later, little Eddie slipped out of show business
and became a tree stump. Just kidding, Eddie fans; I think he
must have had something Preminger wanted, but one feels sorry
for Henry Fonda having to do the acting for both of them, like St.
Christopher carrying the infant Jesus across his shoulders through
the raging fjord.

It's Betty White playing the lone female senator—Betty
White, later on a sitcom star thanks to her petulant goofy parts on
The Mary Tyler Moore Show and *The Golden Girls*. Here she's
unrecognizably young, though not really young, as "Mrs. Adams," a
direct link to America's Federal past, a steely wasp woman armed
with wit and elocution. It's Inga Swenson (Ellen Anderson), as Don
Murray's set-upon wife, who gives the movie emotional strength, as
from scene to scene she grows suspicious of him, first that he has
enemies, then that he's the enemy, and she'll do anything to protect
her "Pidge." The playful scenes in her garden have her caressing
little Pidge in visual pictures that recall the impressionist paintings of
Mary Cassatt; afterwards, as she descends into a sort of madness,
she bursts through the plantation shutters like Medea, crying out that

she'll take little Pidge and leave, Brig, I swear I will! Oddly enough, like Betty White, Inga Swenson went on to sitcom fame too, as the domineering white housekeeper on seven seasons of *Benson*. What this has to say about Preminger's casting prowess I'm not sure, but the Ellen-Pidge scenes in *Advise and Consent* have the sort of naked emotional charge we associate with a Cassavetes or Scorsese,

When Preminger released *Bunny Lake Is Missing* fans were disappointed at his decision to pull back from the big "super-pictures" he had been making—in addition to *Exodus, Anatomy of a Murder, Advise and Consent*, there had been *The Cardinal* and *In Harms Way*—each analyzing, recreating, and deconstructing a different social structure. And Preminger's switch to making a black and white suspense thriller with a decidedly smaller budget and a trim cast—in imitation of *Psycho*, I suppose—felt funny, as though he was trying to do things on the cheap. Where was Jill Haworth, where Peter Lawford, where Burgess Meredith? As I look at *Bunny Lake is Missing* now, however, I see it cut out of the same cloth as the spectaculars, just a little bit further down the register. It's got two great one-of-a-kind stars, Lawrence Olivier and Noel Coward, and two erratic, *sort of* talented Hollywood paper dolls, Carol Lynley and Keir Dullea. (Coward is said to have been rebuffed sexually by the latter and to have dismissed him afterwards as "Keir Dullea, gone tomorrow.") In addition, the redoubtable UK actresses Martita Hunt and Anna Massey play nursery schoolteachers strangely indifferent to the possibility that a child has been snatched from their school. Massey, best known for her parts in *Peeping Tom* and *Frenzy*, here adds a third genre masterpiece to her filmography.

The cast is noteworthy but the best parts of the film are Preminger's imaginative, exuberant and unsparing setpieces, the various social machines Carol Lynley is called on to negotiate. There's the "sanitarium" to which she is taken after a bad blow—you see the complete workings of the place in five or six minutes of incredibly well-chosen shots, and some wonderfully well rehearsed "bit players," extras nearly, who carry forward the burden of exposition with just a few mumbles and disjointed comments. But we hardly even notice this deft background because of the high drama of the foregrounded situation, Lynley's attempts to escape the mental ward by hook or by crook. Watch the reptilian slither with which she extricates herself from her stretcher-bed: she's there, and then with one ugly motion she's on the floor—nearly a whole Martha Graham dance in one little gesture. *Bunny Lake* must have been on Steven Soderbergh's shortlist of films.

Or how about the scene at the doll hospital? For some reason, Preminger constructs not just one set for the "doll surgery," but three—it's probably terribly symbolic, but he has made it have three floors, attic, basement, and main shop, where what looks like all the dolls in London have been lodged on row after row, shelf after shelf, their seeingless eyes meaningless holes onto a meaningless universe, while Lynley searches alertly for a particular doll that used to belong to the missing Bunny Lake. Despite her near breakdown, her search is deft and careful, as methodical as a princess in a fairy tale picking a needle from a haystack. This more than anything else convinces us that she's not as loony as the script wants us to think she may be. Yes, there are gaping holes in the plot, and critics who dubbed the movie "The Logic Is Missing" were right on the mark, and yet Preminger's minute examination of these weird English institutions has a fascination all its own. Best of all, I expect, is the "Little People's Garden School" that dominates the early reels of the film, the strange "First Day Room," the "threes" and the "fours," Anna Massey's defiance and unhelpfulness dissolving into tears after Keir Dullea buzz saws his way through her false front of propriety. Then the bizarre search up, up into a staircase that leads into the secret flat of ex-headmistress Ada Ford (Martita Hunt), with her collection of taped children's voices that would probably land her in prison today. There's not a wasted minute or word in *Bunny Lake Is Missing*, it is one of my favorite films of its era, and as an added plus the Zombies are outstanding! The fangirl in me screamed when I saw them on the pub TV. And among their three numbers, my favorite, "Just Out of Reach," a telling comment on the narrative of *BLIM*, though I guess it could have been "She's Not There."

Preminger brought back the super picture in *Hurry Sundown*, which painted on a large scale a theme briefly touched on in *The Cardinal*—the effects of racism and class struggle in the American South. By now Preminger had fallen out of favor with the critics, and he was reduced to playing Mr. Freeze on the American TV hit *Batman*. He was notorious rather than revered and, in *Skidoo* (1968), Preminger took on hippie attitude and made a notorious flop, though a recent comeback of this little-seen title has been proof positive of his genius for mise-en-scene and everything else. Maybe it's just me, but when critical opinion describes a director as "desperate," that's when I get my party started. John Philip Law and Alexandra Hay make a stunning young couple, as he explains to her in the roomy front seat of his used Rolls, "If you can't dig nothing, then you can dig anything— you dig?" He's so persuasive and suave, I find myself nodding thinking about how far I am from a proper understanding of nothing, but if only I had "Stash" to explain it to me parked by the curb in front of my parents' house, I'd attain spiritual enlightenment absolutely. Carol Channing flutters about, while Jackie Gleason rushes out, drags Stash from the car, and knocks him to the lawn. "You will not marry my daughter!" Alexandra Hay explains, "Hippies don't believe in marriage!" to which her dad retorts, "What is he, a faggot?" Gleason, with his probing questions, acts as an analyst John Philip Law, flat on his back in the grass, is the analysand. "Violence is the sign language of the inarticulate," he pronounces carefully, as though willing everyone in the world, particularly Robert McNamara and Lyndon Johnson, to heed his words. Yes, it's sort of campy but it's played much straighter than you can imagine. Soon there's a body painting scene inside a hippie VW van that casts the youthquake experience in soft, glowing, pastel colors and everyone is beautiful—the van's large enough so that Hay and Law and about a dozen other hippies can stand comfortably, embrace comfortably, paint each other's bodies in detailed and firm strokes, while an older woman, seated on the left hand tire guard, sings a pure, aching version of "Johnny, We Hardly Knew Ye." In classic Hollywood cinema the archetypal bodypainting scene has always been George Sidney's *The Swinger* (1966), four of five guys sending Ann-Margret, half-naked, poised like a dancer, gliding along the floor through pools of pink, white, red paint. But *Skidoo* is a more thoughtful and meditative film than *The Swinger,* kind of the Claude Autant-Lara to its Roger Vadim.

I had dinner some years back with the writer and critic Franklin Bruno, who was then writing a biography of the lyricist John Latouche. Bruno had recently contacted a Carol Channing impressionist who swore he could get Carol a message. My god, wouldn't that be something to interview Carol Channing? What glamour! What longevity! And yet what a limited appeal, is there any show business personality with so few real fans? I only got to like her last month, I mean got the chance to see behind her legendary freakishness. Dodie asked Franklin if he had seen *Skidoo* for she had suffered, agog, through many of its key sequences in a rare recent screening, and fantastically enough Franklin responded with a full-bodied rendition of Channing singing the title number, written by Harry Nilsson and surely one of the weirdest songs in the world. She sings it while mounting a yacht with a crew of rowing hippies, and she's wearing a three-cornered hat and the brocaded jacket of a Revolutionary War general, except cut from vinyl by 60s fashion superstar Rudi Gernreich. I felt close to Franklin Bruno then, very close. You have to hand it to a guy with balls enough to sing "Skidoo" to a table filled with poets ignorant of, or frankly averse to, Carol Channing's difficult genius.

When you deal with Otto Preminger there's possibly too much story to deal with in one volume, so the 2008 *Otto Preminger: The Man Who Would Be King* by veteran journalist Foster Hirsch suffers from NEI—not enough information, though it's hundreds and hundreds of pages long. One might ask for a whole book just on the relationship between Preminger and Jean Seberg, for their back and forth intimacy, the sense that they ruined each other in a way, is something Hirsch works up perfectly, and for once he seems to have informants in all the right places and with the proper combination of critical judgment and insider information. One is encouraged to think of *Saint Joan* and *Bonjour Tristesse*—back to back flops for wounded Preminger--as two sides of a single coin, a coin with a profile of short haired Seberg on each side. You're left thinking of her as a proto Edie Sedgwick, Preminger as an irascible Warhol, and the *Saint Joan/Tristesse* one-two punch as their own *Inner and Outer Space*. Preminger seemed to leap away from his infatuation or whatever it was he had for Seberg with the same alacrity with which Hitchcock dropped "Tippi" Hedren after *The Birds* and *Marnie*—so you know there was something big going on, something dangerous and torchy.

Preminger's affair with Dorothy Dandridge might equally well have been expanded. Hirsch credits Preminger as a proto-civil rights pioneer, pointing to Avon Long's often overlooked turn in *Centennial Summer* as just the sort of music number which

Hollywood should be proud of, instead of apologizing for. For every step forward, however, that Preminger seemed to make—placing Duke Ellington on the piano bench alongside James Stewart, for example, even if he had to play Pie-Face, excuse me, Pie-Eyes, or trying to hire Martin Luther King to play a senator in *Advise and Consent,* he takes two steps back. I suppose he should not have discouraged Dandridge from taking the part of Tuptim in Walter Lang's *The King and I*—though a secondary role, a comedown after her starring part in Preminger's *Carmen Jones,* it might have helped preserve her illusion of serious stardom for more than a minute. And speaking of which, how bad can *Porgy and Bess* be? Gershwin estate, release your shroud of silence over this film! It just isn't right to keep it from us, let us judge for ourselves how shrill Sammy Davis Jr can be, how miscast Sidney Poitier.

Big books could be written on so many chapters here—the supplanting of Lubitsch, the Gene Tierney spiral of madness and deceit; the Gypsy Rose Lee affair that led to the birth of her son, Erik Lee Preminger. The big, serious films of constitutional critique each need more pages than Hirsch can possibly give them, even in the deluxe sort of Knopf serious movie bio treatment he gets here. (Around here I think of these thick glossy Knopf books as movie buff porn.) For goodness sake, for a Preminger fan, *The Cardinal* all by itself could use a complete encyclopedia, just for the way the man deployed the little Viennese starling Romy Schneider, her quickeyed grace so sumptuous and moving against Tom Tryon's need to be bigger, need to blow himself up. Though I must say this is the most complete treatment, in and out, that *The Cardinal* is ever likely to get.

What I dislike is Hirsch's need to have something to say about everyone in his path, and he is often vicious as Clifton Webb, which would be fine if you shared his bile and hated his targets as much as he must. Why the hate for the late Ira Levin (who worked with Preminger on the screenplay for *Bunny Lake Is Missing*), why dismiss a great novelist as a "mediocre" hack, it's just gratuitous sniping, and it leaves you wondering why--perhaps an ill Levin refused the biographer an interview? Jackie Gleason is "humor-free" here, while Groucho Marx is "gross, uncouth, extremely unpleasant." Kim Cattrall will want to go into hiding after the full-scale attach Hirsch mounts on her. Not that I'm a fan of Kim Cattrall, but still! Give the girl a break! As for Dyan Cannon during the filming of *Such Good Friends*, well, I wasn't there, but neither was Hirsch and he paints her as worse than Grendel's grandmother. And Romy Schneider? Loveable, pathetic, ravishing Romy? I refuse to believe that "Romy really was an awful person," "high-strung and arrogant," etc and an impossible demon. No way Jose! Even Ursula Andress comes off as a shrew, and there's no evidence Preminger ever spoke to her, so it seems that Hirsch just delights trashing all these women just because it's easy.

OK, so now *Exodus* looks like the craziest movie ever made! And perhaps the one with the deadliest afterlife. The question is, does it damn Preminger forever, like the late Cantos Pound?

Due Process
(With A Pinch Of Sugar)

☆

John Olson

Apropos Jimmy Inkling, a novel by Brian Marley
Brighton, England: grandiota, 2019

Who doesn't love a courtroom drama? The intense, concentrated
effort to establish guilt or innocence, to get to the bottom, to
subdue that wily animal known as the truth in a cage of eloquence
and incontrovertible evidence. Each case is a charged theatrical
performance of high emotion, tearful confession, skillful elocution,
and brilliant (or fumbling, as the case may be) legal strategy.

One of my favorites is *Witness for the Prosecution* with
Charles Laughton, Marlene Dietrich, Tyrone Power and Elsa
Lanchester. This drama is chock-a-bloc with surprising twists
and turns and bitter ironies. Human nature is put on display and
shown to be capable of pulling off spectacular deceits. Another
great cinematic trial is 1982's *The Verdict*, in which seasoned,
hard-drinking Paul Newman – down on his luck after being fired
from his previous prestigious Boston legal firm for jury tampering
– encounters one seemingly unsurpassable obstacle after another
and yet hazards a huge risk in taking a highly squishy case to trial.
The quest for the truth here is full of throttling difficulties, sexy

entanglements and ponderous disincentives. It's inspiriting to watch Newman's case-hardened, whiskey-guzzling attorney persist against the odds and find redemption along the way.

Apropos Jimmy Inkling is a very different kind of courtroom drama. For starters, the courtroom isn't a courtroom: it's a cafeteria. A man - identified simply as a customer - is buttonholed by a mysterious identity who begins questioning him about a nefarious character named Jimmy Inkling. The customer, patient but confused - and all the more flummoxed upon being told he is a "witness" in a trial - tells his perplexing but resolute interlocuter that "I came in here on the not unreasonable assumption that this was a café. That's what's written on the sign outside, and there's nothing but café paraphernalia in here. The predominant smell is of coffee, not periwigs and dusty legal tomes. Look, on every table there's a laminated menu and a defanged rose in a glass flute. Over there, chalked on a blackboard, a list of lunchtime specials. Paper napkins in a stainless steel dispenser. Sugar in a bowl. This is definitely a café, not a courtroom."

But wait, there's more: turns out the customer is no ordinary customer but a decade ago was a contestant on a TV quiz show called *Mastermind* and whose special area of expertise was "The History of Inkling Inc., 1967-2007." The customer's presence here is not, after all, completely arbitrary. The vigorous, elfish prose animating this dialogue implies eddies and swirls of impending abnormality. A few references sprinkled in to places like Haydock Park and a West End drinking club suggest that we are in England. Information about a vasectomy to be performed – as a favor - on the interrogator's daughter's "unsuitable boyfriend" suggest more than an inkling of unsettling behavior.

Clearly, this is no formal, ordinary legal proceeding. Nor is this an ordinary novel. It proceeds by dialogue alone, à la the Socratic dialogues, but with less polemic and more panache and improbability. A robust blend, shall we say, of Guy Ritchie and Monty Python.

The accused – although no formal charges have been stated – is a larger than life criminal kingpin named Jimmy Inkling, who isn't present at the proceedings. Everything we learn about the man is the stuff of legend. "In the rotten heart of the criminal underworld, hidden from the prying eyes and ears of various law enforcement agencies, Jimmy Inkling is king. The man to go to if you want something done. The fixer's fixer."

The man I picture (this being England where – according to the testimony of the gravedigger in Hamlet, no one will know if Hamlet is crazy because "everyone there is as crazy as he is"), is Ian McShane as the criminal kingpin Teddy Bass in *Sexy Beast*, specifically the demented, murderous, psychopathic fiend McShane brought fantastically to life in expertly tailored clothes and the twisted erotic pleasures in which he indulged, particularly when he was engaged in his favored pursuits of bullying and manipulation.

There are also inklings of Donald Trump, as Jimmy Inkling, among his other dubious gifts as a criminal kingpin, was once the star guest of a reality TV show.

The trial that runs the full length of this novel is an ongoing portrait of Inkling (he comes to us in inklings, but also signs, tip offs, expositions, intimations and dead giveaways) and as the information accrues Inkling's profile becomes increasingly vivid and maddeningly ambiguous. Which is all the more curious – and haunting and weird – because he's absent from his own trial. He may not even be alive, though no one knows for sure.

Marley's novel isn't about establishing a state of guilt or innocence or solve a murder mystery as to examine and showcase (with abundant humor) our will to verify a single, absolute, unequivocal truth. This is an impossible ideal to fulfill, one which requires - as Nietzsche describes in *Beyond Good and Evil* – "some extravagant and adventurous courage, a metaphysician's ambition to hold a hopeless position," and whose need for resolution "may participate and ultimately prefer even a handful of 'certainty' to a whole carload of beautiful possibilities; there may actually be puritanical fanatics of conscience who prefer even a certain nothing to an uncertain something to lie down on – and die."

This isn't to suggest that we jettison our moral faculties. We need them. Morality doesn't exist in nature. We need ethical values to live comfortably together in our absurdly large and hopelessly complex societies. But to capture a single unconditional perspective – a positivistic teleology intended to fit everyone into the same procrustean bed – is (according to Nietzsche) to throw "pale, cold gray concept nets" "over the motley whirl of the senses."

Or, as Marley states in his novel, "we don't always know

what we don't know."

That's really what's on trial here: consciousness, perception, noesis, epistemology, prepossession, methodological analysis. The will to power, the seduction of words.

The language in this book mercifully avoids any form or shade of legalese. The language is lively, colorful, ebullient and fun. It's full of wit and imagination, myriad asides and an encyclopedic revelry in arcana, the kind James Joyce reveled in in *Ulysses*. Did you know, for example, that C.S. Lewis was a tegestologist? A tegestologist is someone who collects beer mats or coasters. Or that the hardest substance in the world is wurtzite boron nitride? Or that "Liver fluke, worms, footrot, trypanosomiasis, east coast fever, brucellosis and foot and mouth disease are significant problems for the South Sudanese cattle herder"? This is all pertinent to the trial, Jimmy Inkling being a man of considerable means, proportions, fables, components, colors, circulars, exhilarations, exhumations and probes.

And I reiterate: he isn't there. He's wired up to a life support machine at another location.

The trial is conducted by gods who have both god names and (for the sake of convenience) human names. The god whose name is spelled with three squiggles (~~~) (they're actually tildes, as in waltzing tilde)) is also called, appropriately, Mr. Squiggle. He does the bulk of the questioning and appears to be the chief prosecutor.

These gods aren't quite what you might imagine, assuming the form of clouds and swans to rape women or riding chariots pulled by fire-breathing steeds. Their powers aren't quite that extensive or colorful, but they are unique. The third witness, Mr Taylor, whose god name is (roughly) $\Delta\approx\Delta\Delta\Delta^\circ\leq$ (I don't have all the symbols required) has, as a key task in his armory of powers, the ability "to slow the Rate of Depletion in Inkjet Printer Cartridges." I might just burn some incense and try invoking this god with some prayer because my inkjet cartridges are always running dry, a phenomenon I find quite suspicious because I rarely use my printer anymore. I think the ink just dries up. And, as anyone knows, these cartridges aren't cheap.

"Also," $\Delta\approx\Delta\Delta\Delta^\circ\leq$ continues, "Scansion as applied to Wills, Government Documents, Contractual Small Print for Electrical Appliances, Academese and, hardest of all to deal with, the baroque gibberish known as Artspeak (i.e. curatorial and critical writings on the visual arts)." "To my considerable relief,"

> ...poetry and the poets themselves were hived off to another god. Hers is a thankless task, poets being notoriously difficult to deal with, maddened by words, perpetually drunk on them, and given to extravagant and unpredictable behaviour. Like toddlers, really, but with adult vices. Endangerment of self and others is often an issue. Byron set the template for such things. But that's not the worst of it. Their verse: ugh. Almost without exception: ugh. Such mangling and mauling of language. The words weep as poets bend them grotesquely out of shape and crack their tiny bones.

It should also be stated emphatically, unequivocally and a shade nihilistically, that the proceedings of this trial are futile. A fourth witness, Paul Honeyman, is presented as Jimmy Inkling's "unofficial biographer." Remarking on the veridicality of informants, he avers that it's impossible to know for sure. He broadens the case philosophically and submits his judgment regarding the ontological nature of truth itself as an ultimately futile and chimerical pursuit.

> But the simple fact is that truth is elusive and often, despite our best efforts, nowhere to be found. That's why most biographies – even those written by a number of my esteemed colleagues, some of whom are also dear friends – are fact-like semi-fictions that try, with bulldozer rhetoric and masses of superfluous detail (i.e. padding) to convince the reader that they portray their subject accurately in the context of our shared reality. As for autobiographies, they are, almost without exception, fiction masquerading as fact. Fun reads, nothing more. Everyone in the publishing industry knows this. Most readers do, too.

Among the arsenal of gems in Jimmy Inkling's criminal mastermind toolkit is a labyrinth of mirrors referred to as his "funfair labyrinth at Canary Wharf." This is a passage somewhat redolent of Raymond Roussel's strange inventions in *Locus Solus*. "It occupies,"

Taylor describes, "an entire floor of his suite of offices. Or perhaps two floors, it's hard to tell."

> Accessible only by a private lift from his inner sanctum, it's a thing of snakelike undulations, forking paths, dead ends and sudden drops. The lights go out briefly every few minutes and in pitch darkness the walls glide into new, unpredictable configurations. There are no doors other than at the beginning and end, though the end may also be the beginning and vice versa. The walls are lined throughout with distorting mirrors salvaged from funfairs and theme parks the length and breadth of Europe. And not just the walls; there are mirrors on the ceiling and the backs of the doors. Even the floor is mirrored. Once the door has closed behind you there's no way of telling what's where or even which way is up. Take two steps and you'll be lost forever, though your chances of living to see another day are small. Even to peer into the labyrinth from the doorway is a dangerously disorientating experience.

I had an experience not unlike this earlier today, at the Thornton Place underground parking lot. I thought I'd never get out.

Inkling uses his demonic labyrinth "to punish members of staff who have, in his menacingly bland phrase, 'failed to give satisfaction'; and anyone else who incurs his wrath, deliberately or otherwise."

When Inkling judges "that the punishment is equal or equivalent to the offence…the victims are either led or stretchered to safety by the Retrieval Squad – blind employees, hired in compliance with the Equality Act 2010 – and placed in the recovery room,

> …a womblike space of replicated orbicular muscle, loose, soft and blood warm, with filtered light and comforting womblike sounds, from which some of the labyrinth's victims flatly refuse to leave and have to be dragged out by a burly obstetrician using adult-size forceps. Should a forceps delivery by unachievable, there's a caesarean zip.

As these two passages suggest, what we have here isn't so much a courtroom drama, or (in the immortal words of Strother Martin as the Captain in *Cool Hand Luke*), "what we have here is a failure to communicate." Legal niceties aren't as apropos here as the wriggle of words in the semantic arena, which is far more fun than the stern, wood-paneled confines of a courtroom. A cafeteria is more apropos to the phenomena convened in this book, Inkling aside, and a brilliant subpoena for those pariahs of the modern world called readers.

Flying Without Wings

☆

John Olson

Wild Metrics, a novel by Ken Edwards
Brighton, England: grandiota, 2019.

"Memories are fractal," states the author and narrator of *Wild Metrics*, "the more you focus in and magnify them, the more self-similar structures appear in their interstices, that is, in the gaps between them; and then magnifying those further reveals the even more remotely embedded memories in between them that were hitherto inaccessible."

     Fractals are particularly useful in modeling structures such as snowflakes or eroded coastlines; they provide an effective way to find patterns amid random or chaotic phenomena such as fluid turbulence, the formation of galaxies, or – in this instance – the interlacing brocades that constitute the life of a young man seeking both a livelihood in England in the mid-to-late 70s and a livelier, more innovative poetry than what was offered in the literary culture of that time. Finding employment is never much fun, no matter where you live, but if one's proclivities are primarily literary, the problem of generating an income can be particularly thorny. Remarkably, one of the employment opportunities to present itself to K – the "fictional" stand-in for Ken Edwards, with its echo of Kafka's Joseph K – is that of tutoring Paul McCartney's thirteen-year-old stepdaughter, Heather.

This is not stated categorically within the novel. And it is a novel, not a memoir. *Wild Metrics*, like many autobiographical novels, is a *roman à clef*: McCartney is referred to as the Rock Star and Heather is given the name Buttercup. Is it possible the Rock Star could be some other high-profile British rock star with a teenage stepdaughter? Sure. But the details make it evident this isn't Johnny Rotten and his stepdaughter Arianna Forster.

Nor does Sir McCartney occupy a prominent place within this novel. He's basically just K's employer. His appearances are fleeting and politely affable. The real subject of *Wild Metrics* is poetry: what is it? Where does it come from? How does one make it come alive? How does one free it of convention and infuse it with the fractious energy and spirited play of invention, combust with spontaneity, create and annihilate meaning, loosen the fetters of the referential and ignite a chain reaction of wild association and semantic collision?

I've often wondered about the poetry scene in England during the late 60s and 70s. It has largely taken a backseat to the overwhelming predominance of France in the formation of postmodern literature, poets and writers such as Charles Baudelaire, Arthur Rimbaud, Stephane Mallarmé, Alfred Jarry, Raymond Roussell, André Breton, Tristan Tzara, Guillaume Apollinaire, Pierre Reverdy, Blaise Cendrars, Isidore Ducasse and Marcel Duchamp to name just a sprinkling of influences have nourished and inspired the principal aesthetics of experimental poetry in the 20th and into the 21st centuries.

American writers such as Gertrude Stein, William Carlos Williams, Ezra Pound, Marianne Moore, Emily Dickinson, Walt Whitman, H.D. and T.S. Eliot have been a remarkable influence on new and innovative poetics that emerged with a vision and a practice contrary to the conventions in mainstream western society, hugely influenced by strictures of enlightenment rationality. But where has England been in all this? The country that produced Chaucer, Shakespeare and the Beatles must certainly have had a pretty vibrant art and literary scene in the 60s and 70s? Right?

The Beatles produced some pretty amazing lyrics during their ten-year run. "A Day in the Life," "Strawberry Fields Forever,"

"Yesterday" and "Eleanor Rigby" (these latter two being authored in whole by Sir McCartney) are impressive for their condensation and evocative power but they're not poetry, they're songs; they're written to accommodate the music. They're by-products of music, not the autonomous splendor that stands as a true dynamic of linguistic voltage, Charles Olson's "high energy construct."

It's remarkably easy for me to relate to *Wild Metrics*, for multiple reasons. I'm roughly the same age as Edwards (older by three years), experienced the same maddening frustrations of pursuing the chimera that is poetry while trying to support myself with a variety of low-level jobs, and had just begun an autobiographical novel about my own trials and travails as a young twenty-year old man evolving in the Bay Area of the late 60s and early 70s. *Wild Metrics* serves as an exciting example of how to navigate the shoals and tombolos of memory, how to locate those archipelagos of lucid recall and break those coconut epiphanies into savory prose.

It was fairly and mercifully easy to find shelter in the U.S. in the 60s and 70s. Even with the very modest amount of money at my command I was able to rent one-bedroom apartments without much difficulty. The situation in England appears to have been similar, with one salient advantage: the advent of a housing association called Patchwork created in 1976 to provide housing for low-income, single people who wished to live communally. The overarching intent was to create a mixed-need community in which individuals with disabilities could live with others able to provide non-professional care and support.

K describes himself at this time as a person "naturally disposed to melancholy" with "dark curly hair" accented by a "vestigial mustache" attempting to achieve "a sort of white Jimi Hendrix effect." "His speech...

> ...was fairly RP [Received Pronunciation: the instantly recognisable accent often described as 'typically British'] with traces of what later became known as Estuary, but there was something not quite right about him. Once or twice, when his ethnic origin had been revealed the comment had been, "Ah, so *that* explains it" (or something to that effect). Lynne had probably wanted

him to be more Hispanic; that was why *she* went off him eventually and took up with a real Spaniard. Or perhaps she had at first liked the idea of a poet, as a romantic ideal – that often happened – then went off him because her idea of a poet and his did not in the final analysis match. They had agreed about Lorca, but she didn't like Ginsberg and had never heard of Olson, much less Tom Raworth, Lee Harwood or Roy Fisher, and didn't seem interested in finding out.

K finds a room in a Patchwork shared house called Sunderland Terrace "where the shabbiness quotient was high." His roommates consist of a couple named Des and June who assume a management role. Des "was jovial, bearded, prematurely avuncular" who called himself Professor Chaos and referred to himself as a "hippie Jew." June worked for a national disability charity. She was "warm and amusing, always reading books and not reluctant to make pronouncements of them" (she made a "grand dismissal of Graham Greene as 'one of those mediocre English writers'"), loved Des and shared his politics, "but was more skeptical, maybe." A man named Sean lived separately on his own in the basement with Dennis the Magic Dog.

"A regular visitor and intermittent resident was Bode, a bearded South African whom Des and June had known when they were squatting in Bristol, and whom they regarded as something of a teacher. He looked like Solzhenitsyn." Bode – who becomes increasingly troubled and psychologically instable – is further described as being skeptical about "scientific objectivity," and as having had become *persona non grata* in his native land for campaigning against apartheid. He urged the necessity and difficulty of living in the moment. He has a room in the house but his family lives in Dover, so Bode travels obsessively between London, Bristol and Dover. However, there are many occasions in which he goes missing altogether. His "absences were usually mysterious, and he was rarely available to do practical work." Bode, like so many others blessed with a poetic soul, has a fugitive-like existence on Planet Earth, and sometimes waddles clumsily about like Baudelaire's albatross on the deck of a ship when too exhausted to fly, a large ineffable spirit trapped in a finite hulk.

K has a romantic affiliation with a 19-year-old woman named Marie, who "introduced joy into his melancholy head. And this joy spread to the spleen and lungs and other vital organs and also outward into the limbs, so that they were all suffused. What a surprise, what a gift." Marie has a history fraught with serious problems, including a previous marriage (she was 16 at the time) during which she gave birth to a boy who – it is first explained, was taken from her to be put in better, more stable care – but is later revealed to have died while she was holding the infant in her arms. She is extremely poor and has meagre belongings.

There are many others aligned with this household, some who live there, some who – like the young man one of the female housemates brings home during a quest to find discarded but useful materials – with "nothing to his name but the clothes he was in, a pound note, and a black-and-white cat he carried everywhere." "He was frequently....

...unable to finish a sentence. Phina and Des made him a cup of tea and spent several hours talking to him in the kitchen, but he seemed utterly scared and paranoid, questioning everything that was said: What did you mean by that? Did you turn on *the* radio or turn on *a* radio? Why did you say hello? He asked to go to the toilet, spent ages in there with the light off, and had to be coaxed out. His cat had meanwhile gone to sleep in front of the electric heater. Eventually, around three in the morning, Des gave up and went to bed (June had been asleep since eleven), and Phina put him in one of the empty bedrooms, where he remained for the rest of the night and did not re-emerge in the morning. At two the following afternoon Des anxiously knocked on the door several times asking if he was all right. He appeared to have barricaded himself in the room with chairs. Eventually, he consented to come out. He mooched around for a while, ate a slice of bread, then picked up the cat, which had been wandering around, and left suddenly....In the early hours of the following morning, before it was light, the doorbell rang. Des got out of bed and went downstairs. It was the young man again, now minus the cat, asking if he could use the toilet. Des told him politely he could not.

Such is the chaos of living in a collective household. K meanwhile hammers out poetry on a portable manual Olivetti typewriter, "sometimes feeding in mimeograph stencils to run off later on the Roneo." The Roneo is a rotary duplicator that uses a stencil through which ink is pressed, and which could be used a low-cost printing press. Which, indeed, it became. This is the machine would aid K (Ken Edwards) in the production of an experimental poetry press that would evolve into *Reality Studios*, a magazine that helped introduce the L=A=N=G=U=A=G=E poets to a British readership.

Wild Metrics is divided into four sections. It is in the second section – aptly titled "Winging It" – that K goes on tour with the Rock Star and his band in the capacity as tutor to Heather...er.... Buttercup. Buttercup's education needs steady, remedial attention. Academically, she's at the level of a seven-year-old. K's role as tutor is given cursory attention. His accommodations, like others in the entourage, are frequently and arbitrarily changed and Buttercup, typical of a teenager, has little inclination to study, particularly when there's so much more going on that is far more exciting. It seems strangely ironic that the writer of such great songs isn't taking her education more seriously, and that a man with evident literary ability isn't better appreciated. On more than one occasion K finds myself stranded without transport in highly dubious parts of town. And one occasion, Buttercup snitches on K, telling her Rock Star stepdad that he swore at her. He didn't, he remembered using the word 'bloody' with reference to a test. The Rock Star upbraids him for this in a quiet but passive-aggressive manner that left me wondering why it hadn't occurred to him that this would be the typical strategy of a teenager to get out of doing her studies. But I'm not her to cast aspersion on Paul McCartney's parenting skills, however much I'd like to take revenge for all the times I had to hear "Uncle Albert/ Admiral Halsey" on my way to a janitorial job in 1972.

One of the qualities that impressed me the most about this novel – aside from Ken Edwards's prodigious memory (I'm assuming he was able to draw a lot of information from a journal he kept during those years) are the marvelous descriptions and the economy of means by which they're delivered. For example, this description of incense smoke is stunning:

A thin line of smoke, barely a thread, stands vertically still, poised on the tip of the joss-stick in its little brass holder on the bottom bookshelf. At the next shelf up its stillness begins to be interrupted; perturbations gradually intervene, it starts to curl in complicated ways and then to flatten itself in front of the books stored there, crawling upward against and caressing their spines before breaking up, losing coherence in a hazy pall gradually thinning to nothingness at the third shelf. It looks as though the books are starting to catch fire.

"If we knew what we were doing we wouldn't be able to do it," K remarks in reference to the creative process in the fourth and final section of *Wild Metrics*. "The work, the piece of music or writing, would already have competed itself before it was ready to. It would already be imprisoning us with its implacable finality." Even in memory, in trying to remember, in trying to piece together a mosaic of fragments, events from a distant past still churning in our neurons, there is never a finality – that buzzword, 'closure.' As Edwards states it on page 194 of *Wild Metrics*: "In memory, the world is created – re-created – every day, every single moment, becoming new again, bringing into existence the possibilities of new futures, in a fluid state, enhancing survival. Memory is a catastrophic breaking-free, a benign catastrophe, if you will."

Quite often it's not merely the interpretation or a deepened understanding that gives remembered events their richness. It's the liberation we discover in the joy of putting words together, the preservation of a space in which words refer to one another without forming a closed structure. The room is dark, but a door has been left open, and the light floods in.

On the Edge of Space:
'the song of fission'

☆

Ian Brinton

One of the most disconcerting aspects of the worlds created by Ken
Edwards is the way in which characters in his novels hang on the
edge of a tangible reality. *Futures* (Reality Street, 1998) opens with
the main character drifting in and out of a zone of terror and 'it was
as though her consciousness oscillated in an increasingly frantic
rhythm before tipping over into chaos':

> one moment the world was constricting her, she could
> touch its four cozy corners (the four corners of her room in
> fact) with her bare outstretched fingers; the next she was
> in a huge starless void between living and dying; and this
> sequence repeated itself with increasing rapidity.
>
> (*Futures* 5)

Squatting in an isolated house, the only survival from a city
redevelopment scheme, Eileen's horizon is rimmed by the
'awesomely beached ocean liners of modern slab and tower block
estates' with their security lights blazing all night as 'beacons against
the grossly imagined unknown'. In this world of vertigo she clutches
onto a roof-top trough which is accessed only by a trap-door in

the ceiling of her bedroom. Lying out there on the roof she can feel 'completely shut off from everything' and for her it is a private domain 'secluded form the city's faraway intercourse'. However, the vertigo is a psychological awareness of the fragility with which we hang onto the Here and Now which defines our life's presence and Eileen is afraid, again, 'of the space in which she finds herself' and her body 'can't touch its boundaries' as 'anxiety wells unbidden out of that space':

> How often has she lain there, centripetally pinned, terrified/ exhilarated by the blue void beneath her? And then it subsides, and she is back in her familiar rooftop pair with the soothing pigeons.
>
> (*Futures* 14-15)

Ken Edwards is interested in Time's fleeting movement and *Country Life* (Unthank Books, 2015) presents the reader with a strange journey into a twilight world of sea and land as we observe two figures moving across a landscape of 'cold, dark matter'. The friendship between two young men, based upon mutual dependence and then betrayal, placed against a socio-political background of unrest, had dominated Flaubert's great novel of 1869, *L'Éducation Sentimentale* and it had prompted its first contemporary literary counterpart in Julian Barnes's *Metroland*. It prompted a second with *Country Life*, a geographical landscape which shifts between the coastal world of Nuclear Power Station based upon both Sizewell in Suffolk and Dungeness in Kent and the different hum of London life. The two main characters in Edwards's novel, Dennis and Tarquin, move towards the aptly-named pub 'The World's End' and there is a finely-tuned moment of humour when Tarquin's abstract ideas are brought to bear upon the Here and Now in terms of sound. Musing upon the reality of the present moment he thinks of his unpublished monograph 'Neo-Marxist Aesthetics and the Marketing of the Moment':

> There's a chapter on this in his book, as it happens. How making it up on the spot is the only methodology that can adequately counter the marketing of the present moment, by deprivileging (his word) its potential for reification. And so on.

> Come the revolution there will be improvisation workshops
> on every street corner, that the working classes will flock to
> avail themselves of.
>
> (*Country Life* 25)

That quiet humour of the sub-clause 'as it happens' contrasts
delightfully with the pomposity of the title of the 500-page book and
brings to mind the tensions between the immediacy of improvisation
and the carefully planned picture of the Future.

Ken Edwards raises a question of some considerable
significance towards the end of the novel after the nightmares have
all unraveled:

> When does night cease to be, and where does dawn start?
> Where does an event end, and the next one begin? But
> there are no events or incidents, only endless flux. A thin
> strip of light cuts the rim of the sea. There's glossy, flat sand
> at the waves' edge. And the waves continually move in, in
> corrugated lines, a long shadow at the base of each and
> white flecks of foam appearing at their peaks; and one after
> another with a low crash each flings itself at the sand and
> the packed shingle above it, pauses, then withdraws with a
> lengthy hiss before the next starts to arrive. The rhythm is
> slow; it does not vary.
>
> (*Country Life* 193)

As both Dennis and the novel's narrator stare out in Arnoldian
resignation at the waves which 'Begin, and cease, and then again
begin' we are left with a world of the 'darkling plain' upon which
'ignorant armies clash by night'.

An earlier contemplation of the larger issue of our existence
in relation to our inherited historical, genetic or moral growth had
led Dennis to raise the simple question of why he and Tarquin didn't
'trash' a helpless old woman who was lost on that bleak Suffolk
coastline:

> This is just a hypothetical question, you understand. What
> stopped us taking advantage of her? Trashing her, I mean?
> What are you saying?

> I mean, she's no use to anyone really, is she? She's a waste of space. In the human food chain, wouldn't you say she's pretty low?
> Yeah, but – that's a pretty weird, big question –
>
> (*Country Life* 26)

When the poet J.H. Prynne read the earlier novel *Futures* he wrote a substantial criticism of it in the form of a letter to Edwards in March 2000 in which he presented his reflections upon reading the novel for the first time. He suggested that 'Only the thin narrow line of the future itself may perhaps be innocent because unknown and unknowing, like the zero point of birth which tells us nothing'. In the world of a less subtle writer such as Anthony Burgess the answer to Dennis's question might perhaps have been presented in the ultra-violence of Alex and his droogs from *A Clockwork Orange*. The whole of Prynne's letter appeared in *Golden Handcuffs Review* 9.

In *Futures* a seeking for a definition of reality is presented to the reader as Eileen (often referred to as Eye) goes to her daily task at the office the morning after killing the man who had raped her on the roof-top. Her job was to sit all day in front of a VDU screen 'entering text not of her own origination'. What strikes one so immediately about this daily activity is its inbuilt sense of pointlessness:

> Although she had never thought about it much before, it now came upon her how strange a way it was to make a living. She fused her consciousness with this small pulse-being that ceased to be and remade itself moment by moment, and created out of this the illusion of permanent reproduction. The reproduction belonged, not to her, but to the company – which, in recompense, paid her so much each month.
>
> (*Futures* 37)

Later in the novel an echoing shadow of this apparent nothingness appears when Eye is confronted by a part of the city that 'teetered on the edge of civilisation'. Cycling away from the dead body on the rooftop she passes through a dark alleyway on the edge of the Thames where she sees 'bodies inert reclining under the bridge'. At once we are faced with what Graham Swift had referred to in his

1983 novel *Waterland* when he suggested that as you turn a corner you arrive at the moment 'where Now and Long Ago are the same and time seems to be going on in some other place'. Living takes one across boundaries which divide the present from the future and in the world of Ken Edwards we seem to inhabit a place where there is no past and certainly no future but 'just the husk that formed around the immediate present' where 'nobody cared.' This sense of immediacy is what also haunts the conclusions that Dennis comes to in *Country Life* as he talks to Alison and tells her that there is no point in worrying about the future because if there isn't one we won't know and so 'we should think of our lives as a succession of present moments'.

Eileen's roof-top sanctuary in *Futures* had been invaded by a confident young business man whose eye was continually on the look-out for a speculative future: the scope for development. Her space above the streets inevitably calls to mind that 'Garden on the Roof' in Dickens's late novel *Our Mutual Friend.* There the invader was the owner of the property and he can only be contemptuous of what has been made of his asset. As Fascination Fledgeby, can only hear the City's roar and be struck by the smoke in the air the hunchbacked Jenny Wren offered a different perspective:

> "But it's so high. And you see the clouds rushing on above the narrow streets, not minding them, and you see the golden arrows pointing at the mountains in the sky from which the wind comes, and you feel as if you were dead."

This sense of freedom and distance from which to evaluate the on-going process of the world finds itself transposed into the more clearly autobiographical prose of the recently published *Wild Metrics* (Grand IOTA Press) as the narrator, K, finds himself in his 'eyrie at the top of the house with its commanding view over the rooftops of London'. As with Eileen's roof-garden this elevation becomes 'a refuge from social interaction'. Before the brutal invasion of the NOW, Eileen's roof-top sanctuary had been 'her paradise garden in the sky, secluded from the city's faraway intercourse.' However, later in the novel as she cycles away from having killed the serpent on the roof-top she meets up with a former lover and as they discuss ideas about Time she says that it's not a garden of Eden she wants but 'a transformation of now'. A similar echo of loss can later be heard in *Country Life* as Dennis walks around the world of the Peninsula and sees the junk piled in 'fields of a ruined Eden'. As an outcast from Paradise Eileen travels through the two days since the expulsion and the style of movement in the writing has become indicative of Ken Edwards's prose:

> The question was too difficult; easier to pedal, one push at a time, one leg and then the other, building up a journey from such small blocks of attention; a voyage of discovery? or invention? Each small focusing of attention contributed to the big focusing, the world coming together.
>
> (*Futures* 111)

By the time we reach the novel's end there is a type of resolution to these questions of immediacy as Eileen takes her child, conceived presumably by her reluctant intimacy with either John I or John 2, back to that desolate house in the city. The narrator can only imagine what that moment might have felt like as
'The smell of the child, its soft limbs, its tremendous, sought-after smile, its cry from the heart' holds Eileen more powerfully even than 'the blue space of the sky above the rooftop'. She watches it now, as it plays with a woolen animal, putting it experimentally in its mouth. As the narrator sees the moment he becomes aware that 'Something is always happening: peaking, then falling away, each a unique event that nevertheless sends out ripples of consequence, for the first and last time'. He can no longer describe these events with their uncertain outcomes and can no longer describe them, 'let alone assess their significance beyond the blank page at the end of this', his 'imagining of her surge of love for the child – and the realization that, after all, she can feel such love.'

Perhaps then an answer to Dennis's hypothetical question concerning the lost old woman on the coast-line marshes may be located in what Prynne was to refer to as the 'narrow line of the future' echoes itself in Ken Edwards's 'thin strip of light' which 'cuts the rim of the sea'. This is where we are and after this there is 'the blank page'.

The authorial voice of *Wild Metrics* tells the reader that memories are fractal:

> The more you focus in and magnify them, the more self-similar structures appear in their interstices, that is, in the gaps between them.
>
> (*Wild Metrics* 10)

In Mathematical terms a fractal is a shape made of parts similar to the whole in some way and the reference to it in this latest book is a reflection of the day-to-day work/world of Eileen as she contemplates her computer screen with its illusion of permanent reproduction. The world in which Edwards's characters move around is one of process, movement, and yet threading its way through the constant changes is a sense of uniformity, fractals. Perhaps it is this sense that Prynne was referring to when he suggested that 'some analysis could be performed, as has for instance been mounted up in respect of Beckett's *Watt*, to map out the latent fault-lines'. The Beckett referred to by Prynne presented a world where 'nothing had happened, with all the clarity and solidity of something' and in Mr Watt's world 'it revisited him in such a way that he was forced to submit to it all over again, to hear the same sounds, see the same lights, touch the same surfaces, and so on, as when they had first involved him in their unintelligible intricacies'. However, what Prynne noted most of all about the style of the writing was what became the most notable feature to his ear: 'the way that your sentence structure so steadily keeps its distance, in cohesional outreach, from the one next about to follow it.'

The world of 'fractals' in the geography of Ken Edwards reveals memories embedded between memories and one is confronted by a sense of vertigo as landscapes move:

> Every street featured at least one skip by the kerbside, yellow, rusting, continually filled with rubble, bricks, planks, furniture, the remaining legacies of dead residents (battered suitcases spilling memorabilia nobody could find a use for), and also daily household rubbish opportunistically and illegally offloaded. Occasionally a skip would be hitched to a trailer by men in overalls and towed away, but soon another would appear in its place.
>
> (*Wild Metrics* 22)

However, any direct sense of autobiographical writing in this latest work of prose which incidentally is subtitled 'A Poem' must be treated with caution and it is worth recalling that when Edwards was interviewed by Wolfgang Gortzchacher in 1995 he pointed out that one of things bothering him about his writing was the 'single point of view'.

> So my current writing does not use the first-person narrative
> at all and the point of view shifts from character to character.
> I found that gives me a lot more freedom, but I suppose
> what I am trying to do is really an extension of what I
> am trying to do in poetry, in that I do some exploration of
> consciousness and exploration of realities.
> (*Contemporary Views on the Little Magazine Scene* 256)

In *Wild Metrics* the area of North Kensington conjured up by the writer is a world of constant change not dissimilar to that which confronts us in Paul Auster's dystopian novel from the late 1980s, *In the Country of Last Things*. In that world 'A house is there one day, and the next day it is gone' or a street you walked down yesterday 'is no longer there today':

> Close your eyes for a moment turn around to look at
> something else, and the thing that was before you is
> suddenly gone. Nothing lasts, you see, not even the
> thoughts inside you.
> (*In the Country of Last Things* 2)

A similar process of movement which is indissolubly bound up with mystery is caught by Edwards as he brings back into view an early poem 'The Circulation of the Light' from the pamphlet of poems *Eric Satie loved children*:

> there is wizardry
> in what manner & by what processes
> stars become dust

Referring to that early collection Edwards had expressed an affection for what was the 'first showing of what later evolved into my preferred procedures: cutting and splicing, juxtaposition, language play, composition by rhythm' (*No Public Language, Selected Poems 1975-1995*, Shearsman Books 2006). As this poem appears again above the horizon in *Wild Metrics* it is read to the narrator's friend Bode whose reaction suggests something central about the whole of Ken Edwards's work:

> ...and Bode responded with great enthusiasm, saying that that was what he meant, that the way the poem had been composed, three lines that had grouped themselves by chance, or chance-enhanced decision, showed its own Process. And there was nothing further to say, because the poem was its own saying.
>
> (*Wild Metrics* 148)

Slowly Becoming Awake
by Hank Lazer

☆

Ian Brinton

In the 'After Words' with which Hank Lazer concluded his handsome
and evocative volume of poems he suggests that the book would not
have had typed transcriptions if it had not been for the publisher's
request for them to be included. Robert Murphy indicated that "he
understood that I would probably consider the suggestion somewhat
heretical, shape-writing being linked to an intentional slowing down
of reading combined with a different physicality of reading (by having
to rotate the page frequently in order to continue reading at all). Also,
there is something about the shape-writing poem that suggests the
motion or dance of thinking itself, perhaps an echo of the dance of
synapses throughout some region of the brain." The movement from
the text on the page to the mind of the poem's reader is referred to
perhaps in the 'Notebook' entry for October 7th 2016:

poem radiating outward   landfall the page

The shaped writing of what is transcribed into this line appears
on the right-hand page of the volume and it describes a gentle
downward curve which might almost be the half of a heart.
   A little over twenty years before this 'Notebook' entry the

poet J.H. Prynne gave a lecture at the Tate Gallery in London on Willem de Kooning's 'Rosy-Fingered Dawn at Louse Point' in which he referred to the painting as being turned about on its axis and "painted in a position 90 degrees from the one which is presented to us now." The visible drip marks left by the overall net rotation through 180 degrees (since the canvas had been rotated 90 degrees to the right and then likewise to the left) left what Prynne described as landscape over-writing suggesting "a curious aspect of variability or even instability to the notion of its axis." In terms of Hank Lazer's sequence of poems arising from a series of 'Notebook' entries this suggestion of movement is powerful in its provocation to keep re-thinking one's responses to what are, after all, quite autobiographical pieces. I am also reminded of one of the moments in Ezra Pound's opening section, 'Terminology', of his 1952 publication *Confucius, The Great Digest & Unwobbling Pivot* in which he refers to 'The process', an ideogram which appears on the right of the page, as "Footprints and the foot carrying the head; the head conducting the feet, an orderly movement under lead of the intelligence."

In an article titled 'Ethical Criticism and the Challenges Posed by Innovative Poetry', published in *Golden Handcuffs Review* in 2017, Lazer had referred to the process of movement in the work of Larry Eigner:

> Larry Eigner's poetry presents us with a perpetual changing of direction, often a swerving from word to word, from line to line. The page becomes a highly malleable (seemingly infinitely so) locale for an instance of grace and mind, a turning about that is highly particular, idiosyncratic (and a perhaps simultaneously universal?) movement of consciousness in a complex relationship with language.

Dated May 29 1971 an Eigner poem cuts forward across and down
the page:

paper

      a cut map

            beautiful

                 land

                       beds

                           tree

                               the air

                                    to dance in

Lazer suggests that innovative poetry changes radically the nature of
the reader's (and teacher's) authority in relation to the text and points
to the "uncertainty, indeterminacy, and necessarily heuristic nature
of such reading" in which "a profound epistemological and ethical
shift" takes place. As readers of *Slowly Becoming Awake* we become
deeply involved in these shifts of perspective and the opening lines of
the sequence dated 30th May 2016 confront us with both the reason
for not starting something new and its opposite, the contemplation of
what lies ahead:

today is not the day to begin something new

    risk of a new notebook

    risk of a different set of pens

death of a young passionate nephew crashing into trees beside the
winding highway not the best day to begin something new   & so it
begins

Threading its way through the downward movement of the opening three-line statement is an upward sweep which begins with the word "death" and we are reminded of a statement Lazer makes at the book's close, referring back to its opening, in which he suggests that *Slowly Becoming Awake* "exists within a broad shadow of death":

> There is the tracking and witnessing of an ongoing sense of loss as my Uncle Stan (neurosurgeon and Biblical scholar – crucial to my own renewed spiritual engagement) experienced the painful decline of dementia and, finally, death.

'Notebook 32' concludes with a visit to Stan's library "while spending time with my Aunt Linda, during a week when I was also taking part in a memorial service at the Getty Museum for my good friend David Antin".

> Then, there is the horrific death of my nephew Jay Parker in his early forties.

Cutting downwards through the whole poem is a sinuously presented question in blue "In what form are the broken pieces manifested?" Ten pages further on a form of answer appears as a manifestation opens upside down "with eyes half-opened before the blank wall" before being followed by s statement the right way up and closer to the bottom of the shape poem

> to know it you must slow down

> > > > & be here   fully attentive.

In that essay on the challenges posed by innovative poetry Hank Lazer sees David Antin as one of America's great poet-philosophers and he quoted Antin in a way that looked forward to this new and fine publication from Dos Madres Press

> > how long is the present?

> > > > > that's a question
> > i have a very strong commitment

i take very seriously as a poet
        to the idea of the present

Re-enacting the Sacred in Robin Blaser's *The Last Supper*

☆

Susan McCaslin

"Marvellous!!" "Astonishing"—two memorable words I heard Robin Blaser utter when I first attended his "Classical Backgrounds" course on arriving at Simon Fraser University in the Fall of 1969 as a raw graduate student. I was a twenty-two-year-old lapsed Presbyterian who had fallen in love with the Romantic poets as an undergraduate at the University of Washington in Seattle, having chosen SFU because of my opposition to the Vietnam War. I arrived with my my draft-resisting boyfriend to make a new life in Canada, drawn to SFU because I had heard it was "a hotbed of radicalism." Soon Robin became my thesis advisor, under whose guidance I worked on the Romantics, Blake, and Coleridge, completing my MA thesis on Edgar Allan Poe's *Eureka* in 1973. I pursued Robin's suggestion that *Eureka* was not a scientific treatise on the origins of the universe, but a long poem, a cosmogonic myth. I had been transported by fairy tales and myths throughout my childhood, but soon learned from Robin more and more about the energizing power of the mythopoetic imagination. Robin asked me if I was Catholic, but I explained that was not the case. Yet as an undergraduate I had begun reading the European mystics like Teresa of Avila and John of the Cross, as well as Dante, and was already drawn to the mystical and esoteric streams of world religions. Later, I learned Robin's father had been Mormon, his mother Roman Catholic, and his beloved grandmother Sophia Nichols, Unitarian. Given how avant-garde and "hip" Robin was, I found it hard to believe he had once been an altar boy. How lucky we are that he pursued his true calling as a poet and educator.

I have raised the ghosts of Robin's childhood to contextualize both his rejection of repressive, dogmatic, homophobic, racist forms of religion and his simultaneous desire to probe to the heart of what he called "the sacred." When I later discovered he had written a libretto in collaboration with the modernist British composer Harrison Birtwistle on the theme of *The Last Supper,* I was intrigued to see how he might have conjoined his rejection of what he called "Christianism," a perversion of the west's central sacred myths and stories, and his sense that aspects of these transformative biblical texts might be reinterpreted and re-imagined.

When I went to the archives at SFU to dig into the materials related to Robin's libretto, I discovered that the opera unfolds a scathing critique of institutional Christianity, yet is simultaneously a revitalizing re-enactment of the events of the biblical story. The figure called "Ghost," a modern, human presence rather than the third person of the Trinity, is sung by a soprano, representing the both the audience and the feminine. She mediates as character and chorus, enabling the disciples and audience to peer though the "three zeros of the year 2000" to examine the intervening violent centuries since Jesus's death. What we see is what Robin calls a "subterranean stream" of bigotry, racism, homophobia, hatred, war. Christ's poignant lament midway through the opera, "The Holocaust shattered my heart," suggests that demonizing the figure of Judas as Christ's betrayer and blaming the Jews for the crucifixion of Jesus, led to centuries of anti-Semitism that eventually erupted in the Holocaust. Robin reinforces this motif by folding in the Jewish Canadian poet A.M. Klein's lines: "Don't you hear Messiah coming in his tank, in his tank?" Here the Christian religion reveals a dark underbelly of totalitarian violence.

Yet other striking aspects of the libretto redeem it from being simply an exposé of how the Christian tradition in the west was co-opted and corrupted by empire and religious power structures. The larger question, "Who is God? What is his name?", raised at the beginning of the opera by the Chorus Mysticus of women's voices is not addressed by linear reasoning. Paradoxically, "God," revealed to Abraham as "I Am" in the Jewish scriptures, is presented as uncontainable by any name, yet is an ontological unity of many "spilled names." God the unnameable mystery is vital presence within and beyond the duality of both being and becoming—an existential otherness, a mystery alive but hidden in the world.

Robin's is a layered mythopoetic text that invites audience participation. The emphasis is on questions, engagement in a fluid Whiteheadian process that doesn't provide absolutist answers. "Who is the betrayer and what was betrayed?" echoes in various voices throughout the opera.

Jesus's insistence, against the protests of the eleven disciples, on reintegrating Judas into the community is a striking departure from traditional interpretations of the story. Robin had explored the Gnostic texts and would have been aware of alternative versions of the canonical accounts through the Nag Hammadi discoveries like *The Gospel of Judas* and *The Gospel of Thomas*. In the libretto, Judas, as in the Gnostic gospel, is presented as acting on what he believed was Jesus' wish. In a moving aria he expresses his regret: "I looked upon his silver face and wept." Jesus also welcomes Thomas' doubt and questions as essential to faith.

Finally, Robin emphasizes Jesus' washing of the disciples' feet, giving it prominence even over the partaking of bread and wine. The latter has been the basis for atonement theology built on the premise that God cannot forgive sin except though the violent sacrifice of his son. The tender washing of the disciples' feet emphasizes gestures of love, inclusion, mutuality and the creation of what Hannah Arendt called "the public sphere." Christ's action establishes the "kingdom of heaven" as a gift economy rather a domain where the powerful dominate through retribution and violence.

I have chosen to focus on Robin's innovative and complex libretto because it continues to address issues critical to this time: fundamentalist religion as the handmaid of corporate capitalism, the alliance of dogmatic religion with totalitarian structures. Yet more significantly, the libretto speaks to the need for a restoration of wonder and curiosity in response to the wisdom hidden in these ancient texts. It reveals how "living the questions," as the poet Rilke put it, rather than providing a closed system of answers, has the potential to awaken the mythopoetic imagination, enabling us to enter a unified field beyond divisiveness and hatred. My hope is that this libretto, which was performed in Berlin, England, Scotland, and Italy, will be remounted (or shall I say "resurrected"?) here in Canada.

— *Delivered May 10, 2017 at a 10-year Blaser memorial, Vancouver, BC*

Taking up Space:
Donna Stonecipher and
the 21st Century Prose Poem

☆

Nancy Gaffield

Donna Stonecipher is an American poet who grew up partly in Tehran, lived in Prague and currently resides in Berlin. She is the author of four poetry collections, as well as essays and translations. Stonecipher is a master of the prose poem, a form which is less visible in mainsteam British poetry than in the US and elsewhere. An admirer of Baudelaire, Stonecipher writes in the French tradition, but equally out of nineteenth century New England, a lineage which originates with the prose poems of Whitman and Emerson, through Gertrude Stein, and the Language writers such as Lyn Hejinian and Rosmarie Waldrop. She demonstrates that for the American prose poet, intellect is of equal importance to the imagination and inner experience. By focusing on Donna Stonecipher, I wish to hone in on the ontological domain of the prose poem, in the sense that it enables the poet to explore knowledge in ways that verse, even free verse, does not.

Model City is an investigation of the intersections between urbanization and the prose poem through connections with philosophy, history, architecture, social theory and linguistics. It comprises 72 prose poems that answer the question posed at the front of the book: 'What was it like?' The answers come in 288 sentences, which cumulatively show the ways the city and poetic praxis intersect, as tensions arise from the poetic persona's encounter with the quotidian and her nostalgia for the past. What is 'the model' city referred to? Might it be Berlin, where Stonecipher lives, or some imagined city? In some of the poems, Stonecipher is in dialogue with Italo Calvino's *Invisible Cities*. Naming is a significant gesture. Choosing not to name emphasizes processes of interaction, like time and duration, as opposed to static, historical characteristics such as identity of place. Stonecipher's cities are *model* cities, not actual cities, and thus it is what something is like, not what something is. The poems employ the formal technique of *mise en abyme*, where an image containing a smaller copy of itself seems to recur infinitely so that the experience of reading the poems is simultaneously familiar and de-familiarizing. Each poem is a sentence as well as a paragraph, both self-contained and fluid, and each poem is comprised of four sentence-paragraphs. Since all of the poems are numbered, not titled, each poem flows into the next. Throughout the series paradox is a main driver of tension. Below is the first poem:

Model City [1]

It was like slowly becoming aware one winter that there are new buildings going up all over your city, and then realizing that every single one of them is a hotel.

It was like thinking about all those empty rooms at night, all those empty rooms being built to hold an absence, as you lie in your bed at night, unable to sleep.

It was like the feeling of falling through the 'o' in 'hotel' as you almost fall asleep in your own bed, the bed that you own, caught at the last minute by ownership, the ownership of your wide-awake self.

It was like giving in to your ownership of yourself and going to the window, looking out at all the softly illuminated versions of the word 'hotel' announcing their shifting absences all over the city.[1]

---

[1] Donna Stonecipher, *Model City* (Bristol: Shearsman, 2015), p. 15.

Numerous paradoxes appear within each sentence. First there is the intimacy of 'your city', the city you inhabit, that is familiar to you, and yet you are unaware of the fact that new buildings are springing up, and especially that each of them is a hotel. There is the intimacy of your own bed, the one you lie awake in, unable to sleep, thinking of all those other beds in the hotel rooms, unoccupied. The reality of ownership (your bed, your house) is in tension with the surreal image of the poetic persona falling through the 'o' in 'hotel'. The use of repetition and recycling of phrases as a rhetorical device adds emphasis, rhythm and an enhanced sense of unease regarding these paradoxical conditions. Moreover, a constant shifting between foreground and background occurs. In the first sentence, the hotel is in the background, and then in the second it shifts to the foreground with emphasis on emptiness and absence. In the third sentence, language occupies the foreground with the 'o' in 'hotel' but it is quickly replaced by the poetic persona's feeling of falling through the 'o' in hotel. Ownership takes the foreground at the end of the third sentence, before recalling language again (in the word 'hotel') and the associative vacancy of the 'shifting absences' that occupy the city (and language). This exchange of foreground and background creates profound disorientation, amplified by the structure of the sentences. Throughout the sequence, 'it was like' is followed by a gerund (in poem 1: *becoming, realizing, thinking, feeling, giving*). Gerunds are nouns formed of verbs. In this poem, the gerunds are based on cognition and sensation, rather than dynamic verbs. Verbs also locate something in time and space, and so by implication if something is happening now, it may not continue to do so, thus the *becoming, realizing, thinking, feeling,* and *giving* are all impermanent states. The sentence is critical to the way the poem works.

The New Sentence

Ron Silliman's essay 'The New Sentence' helps to illumine the structural aspects of the prose poem. The new sentence is not a unit of logic (logic is an illusion) but an independent thing that relates to the sentences that come before and after in complex and ambiguous ways. The New Sentence is relatively autonomous, though a prose poem does provide continuity via repetition, semantic transfer and sound parallelism. In his essay, Silliman quotes at length Gertrude

Stein, who amongst other things, claimed that 'sentences are not emotional while paragraphs are'.[2] In other words, higher orders of meaning occur when many sentences appear. The paragraph organises sentences in the same way as a stanza does in verse. Whereas in verse line breaks provide what Silliman calls 'torqueing', in other words ambiguity and polysemy, in the prose poem it is the grammar of the sentence that does this. In the poem quoted above, each sentence interacts with the sentence preceding and following it. The first sentence of the poem sounds figurative because of the use of 'like'. (It is also reminiscent of the American habit to use 'like' as a filler word). The second sentence, by use of parallel structure in 'It was like' seems to refer to the same content as the first, though it does so by substitution ('empty room' and 'absence' in place of 'hotel'). The third sentence shifts the point of view (a feature of the prose poem) to the perspective of someone falling from a great height, and the 'bed' introduced in the second sentence is associated with 'ownership'. The fourth sentence presents the sequence of the previous one, leading to its ambiguous conclusion. The sentences do not stand in isolation. The use of pronouns, the recurrence of words or synonyms of words, the use of parallel structures, all work together to create a sense of unity. Here's a reformulation of the structure of the fourth sentence to a lineated version:

It was like giving in
to your ownership of yourself
and going to the window
looking out at all the softly illuminated
versions of the word 'hotel'
announcing their shifting
absences all over the city.

Although my line breaks are arbitrary, this reformulation shows how the meaning changes when the same words are combined into a longer string of words (a sentence), where pace, rhythm and meaning derive from the sentence, not from lineation. As Ron Silliman states, the New Sentence is a perfect vehicle 'for hallucinated, fantastic and dreamlike contents, for pieces with multiple locales and times squeezed into a few words'.[3]

---

[2] Gertrude Stein, *How to Write* (Mineola, NY, 2018) [np].
[3] Ron Silliman, *The New Sentence* (Berkeley: University of California Press, 1977), p. 81.

What is the prose poem?

The prose poem never really caught on in Britain, but it is currently undergoing a resurgence aided by two publications in the last year. Jeremy Noel-Todd recently published *The Penguin Book of The Prose Poem* with ten 'essential' examples. Initially well received, later reviewers have remarked on its 'inability to read poetry' accounting for 'many—the majority—of the selections in the anthology, which is a dismally uneven gathering, demonstrating a fatal lack of taste'.[4] Donna Stonecipher, for example, doesn't appear in it. Neither do many of the other excellent writers of the form: Luke Kennard, Patricia Debney, Elisabeth Bletsoe, Ian Seed, Peter Riley, Geraldine Monk and Alan Halsey. The second publication is *British Prose Poetry*, edited by Jane Monson, containing twenty essays on the British prose poem. This is the first collection of essays devoted to the prose poem, which recounts both its history and its reception.

The popular view is that the prose poem originated in France with Aloysius Bertrand's *Gaspard de la Nuit* (1842), followed by Charles Baudelaire's *Petits Poèmes en prose* (1869), through Rimbaud, Laforgue and Mallarmé to Gertrude Stein and the Surrealists. In the Preface to *Le Spleen de Paris* (1869), Charles Baudelaire defines the genre as: 'the miracle of a poetic prose, musical though rhythmless and rhymeless, flexible yet rugged enough to identify with the lyrical impulses of the soul, the ebbs and flows of reverie, the pangs of conscience'. Crucially, he elaborated his vision of the relation between the prose poem and the city: 'It was, above all, out of my explorations of huge cities, out of the medley of their innumerable interrelations, that this haunting ideal was born'.[5]

In the same way that free verse liberated verse from meter and rhyme, the prose poem eliminated the line as the unit of composition. The emphasis in the prose poem is on the sentence. Not quite prose, and not quite poetry, it is seen as something in between, a hybrid form, paradoxical and subversive. As David Lehman points out, in France it quickly became a genre, liberating French poetry from the tyranny of the alexandrine.[6] While the prose poem in France quickly

---

[4] Craig Raine, Ann Pasternak Slater and Claire Lowdon, eds., 'Our Bold,' *Areté*, 58 (2019), p. 69.
[5] Charles Baudelaire, *Paris Spleen*, trans. by Louise Varèse (New York: New Directions, 1947), pp. ix-x.
[6] *Great American Prose Poems from Poe to the Present* ed. by David Lehman (New York: Scribner Poetry, 2003), p. 18.

gained the status of a genre, it never gained that status in English, and particularly in Britain, where its progress was hindered by T.S. Eliot, who rejected the terms 'prose poem' or 'prose poetry' altogether, preferring to call it 'short prose'.[7]

Admittedly, the term 'prose poem' causes confusion, especially for those who still think poetry is equivalent to verse (standard lines with rhyme and metre). A number of other labels have been suggested, for example, poetic prose, but the term 'poetic' is problematic for contemporary poets because of its emphasis on metaphorical language, stylistic flourishes and lyric intimacy, which are not necessarily characteristic features in poetry of the late 20th and early 21st centuries. Other labels have been suggested: prosaic poetry, but 'prosaic' suggests plodding poetry with a lack of imagination. For poems with a narrative element, short-short story has been suggested, but not all prose poems contain a narrative element. For readers who are interested in matters of definition, I recommend Michel Delville's (1998) *The American Prose Poem: Poetic Form and the Boundaries of Genre*. In this essay I embrace the term prose poem as an intertextual genre differentiated by its tendency to be investigatory, spatially innovative, aesthetically and socio-politically informed. As Delville argues there are as many types of prose poems as there are practitioners.[8]

Prose Poetry and the City

Stonecipher's monograph *Prose Poetry and the City* (Parlor Press, 2017) is an important book on the 21st century prose poem. In it Stonecipher concentrates on the theoretical 'reverberations' that have occurred through a multidisciplinary exploration of philosophy, linguistics, history, architecture, social theory and their relationship to the prose poem. As she writes in 'Preliminaries', Whitman 'invented' the prose poem in the US (*Leaves of Grass*), contemporaneously with Charles Baudelaire (*Le Spleen de Paris*) in France. These two poets, writing in the middle of the nineteenth century, developed a new structure to explore the rapid industrialisation and urbanisation transforming two of the world's great cities into 'long, uniform blocks'

---

[7] Michel Delville, *The American Prose Poem: Poetic Form and the Boundaries of Genre* (Gainesville: University of Florida Press), pp. 5-6.
[8] Delville, pp. 5-6.

(Paris) and 'tall vertical skyscrapers' (New York).[9] As evidenced in *Model City*, this affinity intrigues Stonecipher and drives her investigations into the nature of the prose poem and its interrelations with other poetry and disciplines. The prose poem, Stonecipher demonstrates, needs to be understood enthusiastically. As David Herd writes, 'To be in the mental state of enthusiasm is to be ready to receive words, intimations and ideas, but it is also to be in a state to pass them on'.[10] In the first half of the book, Stonecipher sets out the history and theory of the prose poem. Taking two cities, Paris and New York, she compares and contrasts their development in the 19th century. Haussmann's redevelopment of Paris took place 1850-70; it emphasized horizontality and uniformity, along with those features which make a city liveable—trees, parks and promenades. His scheme eradicated the slums, but also the individual dwelling, amplifying the collective over the individual. The city grid system facilitated the developer's desire to divide the city into tidy plots in order to house as many people as possible. In New York, the scheme was to build vertically, but vertical schemes are hierarchical. Skyscrapers isolate. These two styles of architecture lead Stonecipher to interrogate the rupture that occurred in formal poetry in both places at this time.

Her project in *Prose Poetry and the City* is to put the pieces together in a way no one has done before. The pieces she assembles include De Certeau's 'Walking in the City', Roman Jakobson's essay 'Two Aspects of Language and Two Types of Aphasic Disturbances', Georg Simmel's 'The Metropolis and Mental Life', as well as Jonathan Monroe's work on the prose poem, Walter Benjamin's *The Arcades Project* and *The Writer of Modern Life* (on Baudelaire), Immanuel Kant and Edmund Burke on the sublime and others too numerous to mention here. She begins with De Certeau standing atop the World Trade Center. This is a panopticon view which allows the viewer to observe those below without them knowing. As an architectural feature, the panopticon (a central tower surrounded by cells in a prison) is attributed to Jeremy Bentham, and in the 20th century, the term has been used as a way to describe surveillance in disciplinarian societies. Thus, the city is a 'double-city' consisting of both the concept-city and the lived-city. By the fifth chapter, Stonecipher begins to draw an

---

[9] Donna Stonecipher, *Prose Poetry and the City* (Anderson, South Carolina: Parlor Press, 2017), p. 6.
[10] David Herd, *Enthusiast! Essays on American Literature* (Manchester: Manchester University Press, 2007), p. 5.

analogy between De Certeau's concept-city and the form of a poem. The paragraph is a representation of written thought, as a map is a representation of the city. Both the city and the prose paragraph are spacious, allowing its flâneur/reader to 'meander'. The paragraph on the page resembles the storey of the urban block, which also allows room to drift. De Certeau also claims that there is a rhetoric of walking: 'The act of walking is to the urban system what the speech act is to language'.[11] He bases his argument on structural linguistics, and especially the two concepts of *langue* and *parole* and the two axes of language: paradigmatic and syntagmatic. Sausurre introduced the two concepts of langue and parole in his *Course in General Linguistics* (1916), an investigation of language as a structural system of signs (semiotics). He distinguished language (*langue*) as the general system and speaking (*parole*) as an individual activity. Language lies on the border between thought and sound and in combination these produce communication. In analyzing a text, Saussure was interested in the systemic relationships between a signifier and a signified. Meaning arises from the differences between signifiers. The syntagmatic presented as the horizontal axis is that of combination (*this* and *this* and *this*). The paradigmatic is presented as the vertical axis and is that of selection (*this* or *this* or *this*). Syntagmatic relations combine; paradigmatic relations differentiate, and this has implications for the prose poem.

As Stonecipher argues, *langue* and *parole* are analogous to the concept-city and the lived-city in that *langue* refers to the language system in its totality, and *parole*, the individual's chosen speech (speech acts). Just as we make utterances as part of our everyday interactions with people, the walker interacts with the city streets and its landmarks to find her way. The concept-city influences the practices of the user in the same way that *langue* (the general system of languages) influences the speaker. But, as I shall explain below, this focus on *langue* over *parole* does not address the sentence, because it does not separate writing from utterance. De Certeau envisaged the legal, civic and administrative aspects of the city as contiguous and horizontal, like the syntagmatic axis of language—things which occur in combination (paratactically). The paradigmatic (vertical) axis is the axis of selection and substitution. Thus, as Stonecipher shows, the

---

[11] Michel DeCerteau, *The Practice of Everyday Life*, trans. by Steven F. Rendall (Berkeley: University of California Press, 1984), p. 97.

flâneur poet walking and writing horizontally turns geographical space into prose poetry. Flâneuring is De Certeau's ideal tactic: horizontal walking to achieve vertical 'dancing'. The prose poem uses structures (paragraphs) as an impetus for poetry, just as the flâneur uses the displays in the windows for fantasizing.

Unlike other writers on the prose poem, Stonecipher situates the Language movement in relation to the prose poem in the US. Although the Deep Image Poets (e.g., Bly and Wright) resurrected the prose poem in the 1960s, the Language poets, based in New York City and San Francisco, established its features: disjunction, ellipsis, parataxis, collage, fragmented narrative. Of particular interest is Rosmarie Waldrop and her book, *The Reproduction of Profiles*. Waldrop elaborated the notion of 'gap gardening', which is a metaphor for her cultivation of the liminal. Stonecipher writes in the stylistic heritage of Waldrop, starting with the fact and working towards the idea, combining intimate emotions with philosophical speculation. Both poets, Stonecipher and Waldrop, have centralized the prose poem in their praxis. In the beginning the Language writers were outsiders arguing all art must act as social critique. As a result, much of their early writing is polemical; Waldrop, however, was always more reflective and philosophical, as is Stonecipher.

What can we conclude then from this? Stonecipher sees the prose poem as a product of De Certeau's adaptable human using 'tactics' to navigate her environment. De Certeau differentiates strategies from tactics. Strategies are produced by industrial power, whilst tactics are used by consumers or the non-powerful. Drifting around the city, the poet 'elevates' prosaic events to the status of poetry. But the poem is also like a 'sundial telling the time of [its] history'.[12] In Baudelaire's historical moment the dominant culture favoured prose. Changes in the patterns of life, due to increasing urbanization, economic and social pressures, threatened the very existence of the lyric poem. Georges Lukács wrote in 1923 that capitalism had spread everywhere by the end of the 19th century, where the 'tyranny of the human face' is the only reality. Today the majority of contemporary writers dwell in cities. The city permeates how we live, how and what we write. Added to that are new pressures having to do with the climate crisis, increasing inequality, migration,

---

[12] Theodore Adorno, 'On Lyric Poetry and Society' in *Notes to Literature*, Vol. 1 ed. by Rolf Tiedmann, trans. by Shierry Weber Nicholson (New York: Columbia University Press, 1991), p. 46.

environmental degradation. In these times the subjective lyric poem seems anachronistic and redundant. How will poets address these new challenges in the coming decades?

Transaction Histories

If *Model City* is a mode of enquiry that resonates with the history of urban discourse, then *Transaction Histories* confronts and challenges the dystopias of the present. The book is divided into nine sections. The three poems of 'Persian Carpet' are the first sequence. The Notes section names the word 'abrash', which means the changes in colour and striation that occur in a carpet through the aging process. This is actually a perfect metaphor for the poems themselves. In Islamic culture, it is said that imperfections are woven into each carpet in order that the individual does not offend God: only God is perfect.

All of the poems in the book take up five lines on the page. Sometimes two poems appear on each page, sometimes three; they appear in sequences of six or nine poems. The poems in 'Persian Carpet' uniquely have a caesura (a wide gap) in the third line (echoing Rosmarie Waldrop's notion of 'gap gardening'). These poems explore the possibilities of humour, incongruity and narrative compression. Like *Model City* it builds on the experiments in the urban environment and architecture, and poetically, shifts in point of view, elements of plot and character are employed. Although there are characters, the poems are not character-driven, as in fiction. They exploit the world of objects and of art as a kind of template for the elaboration of ideas. An overarching concern in these poems is a failed relationship and although in this way the poems are anecdotal, as a sequence, they transcend this.

There are four poems titled 'Landscape and Portrait' which all feature a painting or set of paintings by one of the 17th century Dutch masters. In the Landscape section a brief ekphrastic prose poem offers a verbal representation of the poetic persona's encounter with the work of art. The treatment of the painting(s) illustrates how art can disturb the contemporary moment. Then the reader's gaze is re-directed from the painting to a poem titled 'Portrait'. In each of them, container ships are carrying the rubbish discarded by wealthy countries to poorer countries for disposal. Because the departure points and arrival points are named, along with the time of the departure, there is an uncomfortable truth to these poems. Structurally, each of these is a powerful reminder that the page is a space where everything can be seen at once, not just the beauty of the landscape (and its art) but the trash. The final Landscape poem is on Dirck Van Der Lisse. Stonecipher writes:

> The fetishization of nature in eight landscapes around a room is the fetishization of nature segmented into culture, nature deposited into frames at exactly that moment in the general segmenting when nature takes on the tragic dimension of culture, goldenly tamed.[13]

Van der Lisse combined realistic and classical Italianate traditions in his landscapes with sensuous nymphs and satyrs in hazy light. Fetishization is the process of excessive irrationality devoted to an object. Stonecipher seems to be commenting on the commodification of nature via painting, and by extension lyric poetry. The paintings are cultural artifacts that reflect the newly-gained pride in artistic cultural production in the Netherlands in the 17th Century. Similarly, since the Romantic period, lyric poetry has fetishized nature. Stonecipher's 'Landscapes and Portrait' sequence also recalls Marx's theory of commodity fetishism. In 1842, Marx called fetishism 'the religion of sensuous appetites' that trick the fetishist into believing that the object will produce gratification; however, when this fails to happen, the fetishist destroys the fetish.[14] In Stonecipher's 'Portrait':

> Two cruise ships full
> of North Americans on holiday
> round the Cape of Good Hope at 4 a.m.
> dumping garbage along
> the curve

Historically landscapes were treasured by painters and fetishized by the buyers. Our own 'religion of sensuous appetites' sends us scrabbling around the world to visit the rarest and most beautiful landscapes. On average, more than 8 million people fly every day. It is estimated that the average American produces more than 2000 pounds of trash in a year. We believe that our activities will gratify our desires, even as we destroy the planet.

Starting with the fact and working to the idea, Stonecipher

[13] Donna Stonecipher, *Transaction Histories* (Iowa City: University of Iowa Press), p. 79.
[14] Karl Marx and Frederick Engels, *On Religion* (Amsterdam: Fredonia Books, 1955), p. 22.

also combines the personal with the philosophical. The title of the collection, *Transaction Histories*, is telling in this regard. A transaction is an instance of buying or selling something; the action of conducting business, or an exchange/interaction between people. Relationships too are transactional. The opening poem starts: 'Months after the breakup, she wondered....'[15] The dialogic quality of the poems throws light on the couple's two very different ways of perceiving. While the poems are dialogical, their speakers do not necessarily communicate. For example, in 'Found to be Borrowed from Some Material Appearance' 3, Poem 1: 'She even tried to trick her mind into associating the letter 'g' with pleasure, like the silent 'g' in 'sigh,' like the sighs she made under her lover, who did not like to speak during sex'. In Poem 2, 'She knew accidentally saying "reason" when she meant "pleasure" was a bad idea, especially to her silent lover—but there the two words sat, marooned in acoustic shipwreck'.[16] This happens largely as a direct result of the indirect speech mode and the fragmented nature of the discourse. Frequent scene changes and shifting pronouns introduce a variety of speakers and perspectives, which appear and disappear through the poems' revolving doors. Stonecipher's verbal playfulness, puns, homonyms, incongruities and associations all add depth and delight.

<u>Taking up Space</u>

Stonecipher's fascination is with cosmopolitanism and its failures; this is the world we live in now and for the unforeseeable future. In *Model City* Donna Stonecipher recounts the history of urban discourse in order to connect the aesthetics of the prose poem and the embodied experience of the wanderer of urban space. As a primary investigation. Stonecipher's writer-walker is in a continual process of re-negotiation, and through this process, the gap between the architectural structure of the city and the poetic structure of the poem begins to close. Recent work reflects not only the city's vulnerability, but the impact of economic and environmental crises and our response or failure to respond. *Transaction Histories* is in that mold, and its lens widens to take in global relationships, including the possible destruction of ourselves. Both of these collections were written in

---

[15] *Transaction Histories*, p. 3.
[16] P. 65.

the aftermath of the 2001 attacks on the World Trade Center that De Certeau stands atop of, but those who stood atop on September 11, 2001 plunged to their deaths. In the Paris of Baudelaire's day, the homeless were displaced in order that the model city and its arcades could be constructed. In 2019, The Night of Solidarity Project counted 3,641 people sleeping rough, a 21% increase on the previous year.

In his letter to Paul Demeny in 1871, Rimbaud said, 'Inventions of the unknown demand new forms'.[17] Donna Stonecipher's argument that urbanization gave rise to the prose poem is certainly intriguing. The twentieth century radically re-configured concepts of time and space. With Modernism poets developed new 'tactics': experiments in surrealism, Dadaism, sound poetry, graphic poetry, use of collage, simultaneity, to name a few. The prose poem in particular is experimental. As Margueritte Murphy explains: 'Above all the prose poem is a heterogeneous form—not as a simple compromise between poetry and prose, but as a form that almost inevitably brings diverse genres of prose into tension with one another'.[18] It is this tension which is the driving force of the prose poem. For Stonecipher it is the perfect vehicle for capturing the estrangement of the postmodern world and our implication in it.

Works Cited

Adorno, Theodore, 'On Lyric Poetry and Society', *Notes to Literature*, vol. 1, trans. by Shierry Weber Nicolson, ed. by Rolf Tiedemann (New York: Columbia University Press, 1991).

Baudelaire, Charles, *Les Fleurs du Mal*, trans. by Roy Campbell (London: Harvill Press, 1922).

---*Paris Spleen*, trans. by Louise Varèse (New York: New Directions, 1947).

De Certeau, Michel, *The Practice of Everyday Life*, trans. by Steven F. Rendall (Berkeley: University of California Press, 1984).

Delville, Michel, *The American Prose Poem: Poetic Form and the Boundaries of Genre* (Gainesville, FL: University of Florida Press, 1988).

---

[17] Arthur Rimbaud, *Illuminations*, trans. by Louise Varèse (New York: New Directions, 1957).
[18] Murphy, p. 90.

Herd, David, *Enthusiast! Essays on American Literature* (Manchester: Manchester University Press, 2007).

Lehman, David, ed., *Great American Prose Poems from Poe to the Present* (New York, Scribner, 2003).

Marx, Karl and Frederick Engels, *On Religion* (Amsterdam: Fredonia Books, 1955).

Monson, Jane, ed., *British Prose Poetry: The Poems without Lines* (Palgrave Macmillan, 2018).

Murphy, Margueritte, *A Tradition of Subversion: The Prose Poem in English from Oscar Wilde to John Ashbery* (Amherst: University of Massachusetts Press, 1992).

Raine, Craig, and others, 'Our Bold', *Areté*, 58 (2019), 5-151.

Rimbaud, Arthur, *Illuminations*, trans. by Louise Varèse (New York: New Directions, 1957).

Saussure, Ferdinande de. *Course in General Linguistics*, trans by Roy Harris (Chicago: Open Court, 1986).

Silliman, Ron, *The New Sentence* (Berkeley: University of California Press, 1977).

Stein, Gertrude, *How to Write* (1931) (Mineola, NY: Dover Publications, 2018).

Stonecipher, Donna, *Model City* (Bristol: Shearsman, 2015).

... *Prose Poetry and the City* (Anderson, SC: Parlor Press, 2017).

...*Transaction Histories* (Iowa City: University of Iowa Press, 2018).

Waldrop, Rosmarie, *The Reproduction of Profiles* (New York: New Directions, 1987).

---'Why Do I Write Prose Poems (When My True Love is Verse', in *Dissonance (If You Are Interested)* (Tuscaloosa, AL: University of Alabama Press, 2005).

In The Creel Of The Real

☆

John Olson

Heavy Sublimation: New Poems by Leonard Schwartz
Talisman House, 2018. 111 pps.

Often when I read a poem I don't want the poet around. I want the
poem. Not the woman or man that wrote the poem. Ego. Subjectivity.
All that clever rumination one finds in glossy magazines. What I
want is the rumination as it evolves in words, their movement on the
page, or driven by a voice in a room of book-lined walls, or bricks,
where beer is served, and the microphone is on, and we hear words
gathered in art, not playing to the crowd, earning brownie points via
social commentary, but adorning space with wanton association, the
fluid dynamics of a consciousness breaking out in words. I want the
drama inherent in language, not the melodrama of someone using
words calculatedly to coax an audience into applause.

　　　There are exceptions. Frank O'Hara is an exception. He's
everywhere, pouring drinks, dashing back to the typewriter, pounding
out another jungle of words, lianas of tropes. He's exuberant in
the way Whitman was always exuberant, which can be off-putting
to some people. Who wants exuberance when you're looking for
a good clean intelligence to ignite a blaze of association in your

head? The kind of association that leads to dissociation, i.e. trance. Enchantment. O'Hara gets away with it, as Whitman gets away with it, by finding the impersonal in the personal, the objective in the subjective. The energy of their language is as broad and generous as any enchantment, the divine madness we find everywhere in poetry driving pursuits of intellect toward reification, turning predicates into objects.

Which is why I'm often drawn to the objectivists and their fascination with the poem as an object, viola or pickaxe. To see the world clearly and get that clarity on paper. Invigorate it with structure. Match the structure to the material at hand and sculpt it into a self-propagating semantic machine whose moving parts fit like chains and cogs and meshed gears, conveyors of singing gut. These are some of the qualities I find in Schwartz's work, the heavy sublimation alluded to in the title. The immediate pitch of the words sublimating into thought, that strange vapor blowing through our heads, more often than not making a mess of our lives, but sometimes turning into music, dulcet registers of sweetly moving air.

Schwartz's lines are graceful. They move with an exquisitely measured tonality, a twelve-tone simultaneity of possibilities.

I particularly found enjoyment in the series "Poetry As Explanation." There are 12 poems altogether, each a list poem provoked into being by repetitions of the conjunction 'because.' "Because a face that provokes longing, overwhelming / Longing, sometimes expresses comic alarm," remark the first two lines. The surprising element of 'comic alarm' in the second line is typical of the way Schwartz begins to evolve a thought, often with an elliptical spin (nothing worse than an explanation that is overly sure of itself and its conclusions), such as appears in the following two lines, "Because less *retentia* would mean less / Everything that shines later, in the refining." *Retentia* is a Latin word – the source of English 'retention' – though why Schwartz prefers the italicized Latin form is intriguing. I found a reference to it in *The 'Metaphysica' of Avicenna*, mixed with Arabic and Persian nomenclature: "The internal states are subdivided as follows: (1) common sense (*hiss-i mushtarak, sensus communis*); (2) memory (for common sense), *mushawar, retentia.*"

The sense which is evoked is both medical and metaphysical; memory of a face which is so vital it quickly alters expression, and so deepens the experience of being, which is at the core of any spirited work. The theme of desire is distended in the continuing couplets: "Desire's tension dissipates into the acceptance / Of impossibility: that very same tension // Strung just as tightly in place / The next morning, just because." The situation is fractured, a little, by the discordancy of the ways the couplets are structured, which gives them a third-dimensional, sculptural feel similar to the chiseled lines of George Oppen (though it was Williams who began this Cubist approach in his earlier poetry). This is so often the case with desire; it alerts our being to potentials as well as the tensions inherent in fulfilling those potentials, exploring their fuller course, even at the breakfast table, amid scrambed eggs and toast.

"Poetry As Explanation #1" is the only one in couplets. The others unfold their reckonings in columnar, open forms, (the form growing out of the writing process) which occasionally break into stanzas.

There are repeated themes of identity, identity as an entity of deeply puzzling phenomenality, and identity as a driver of desire, "As the primary monologue of the water" sloshing around in us at any given moment. Fluid – fluidity of thought, fluidity of movement – is paramount to the production of these lines. This is evidence of a mind – the mind, taken as a whole, as everybody's problem – glimpsed in its meandering explorations. A telescoping of intentions.

"Because the 'I' can never be institutionalized," he observes, "Entirely, no matter which school / Or residence or group home or enclosure / Is invented for its comfort or edification. / Because consciousness is empty and free. / Because Nature is a frame / One could also call / An eel."

Love that sudden appearance of the eel at the end. I derive great delight from these little jack-in-the-box pop-ups.

Eels are such weird, slippery, primordial little creatures. They swim by generating body waves which travel the length of their bodies, and can swim backwards by reversing the direction of the wave. This makes them ideal analogues for the writing process, tremors of feeling in oscillations of phonemic action. But little? Not always. I misspoke. A 20ft conger eel that weighed 131lb after it was gutted was caught off Plymouth in Devon in May, 2015. It's been proposed that the Loch Ness monster is most likely an eel.

"Because the power snaps off," Schwartz states a few lines down, "With the ease of a bikini top." Thus illustrating the power and elasticity of the image within a linguistic environment of such prodigal allowances.

"Variations On Sane" is a darker, more elliptical work in three-line stanzas. It is a meditation on violence, evil, and the general state of nature in which we find ourselves, odd creatures as we are, with the ability to put our struggles into meaningful sounds. The sentient and the sinister, the innocence and violence of beauty, are put to measure here:

> The blood on a pear
> Attests to the simplest havoc:
> This violent omnipresent.
>
> Were those large raptors
> Or Chinese kites up there
> In the city's cauterizing smog,
>
> On the verge of kissing?
> The way up and the way down
> May well be one
>
> But only the caws
> Of crows
> Penetrate my window.
>
> I don't want to go
> Away! But rain washes
> Everything into the distance.

The multiplicity of contrasting events and images in these lines do indeed – as the poet says – attest to the simplest havoc. Havoc is the omnipresent anyone with a name and a brain must contend with. I think they call it the human condition. I don't want to go away, either. Not forever. Who does? Mortality is a son-of-a-bitch. Poetry – which is the condition language takes in paroxysms of charged emotion -   assumes the instinctual alertness and energy of a woodland animal, spooked by an invisible threat: "Since speech itself / is dependent upon moisture / Sprung from woodland panic."

Schwartz condenses, gets to the meat of a feeling in an

image of the heart as a tyrant, a pounding compression of frustrated appetite: "The heart is fascist / When stonewalled by / The object of its love."

That's a powerful image. It's an ugly feeling when it happens, that magnitude of obsession with someone, their possession and bewitching presence, that maddening inability to prevail, and so bunch into a fascist knot of sorrow and taut force. Love is sometimes the most violent power there is. Tempered by hate.

"Glacier Tale," the final piece of this collection, is a long prose poem that begins with a riddle: "The outside of the inside reveals itself to a special act of reflection."

Inside is so particular in this instance it has its own internal dynamic: "The inside of the inside remains as impenetrable as ice."

That ice should be the central trope of this long prose poem is revelatory of the glistening idiosyncrasies of reflective writing. Insight becomes a divination of ice, "a mimicry of the complex," as Schwartz describes it, "almost as precious as our own lives seem to us in our most precarious moments."

He alludes to two children lost near the peak of the mountain in which the glacier is situated. "The children – a brother and a sister – are very much on their own, singularly in the grip of their predicament, which is that of beings lost in the night."

There is a third intelligence, a mountain god: "A mountain god broods over the possibility of creating free human beings anything but beholden to himself, their troubled creator."

And so the work is a triad, a trinity of incipient human consciousness in the twofold guise of a brother and sister exposed to the overarching enigma of a cold, impersonal colossus: "The mountain is as silent as the mind, as calm as any stone formation without hope for the future, as massive as the night."

The brother is the oldest and takes the lead, although it was the brother that lost the trail. It's the little girl who appears to have the deepest insight: "What she says bears upon the relationship between the visible and the invisible."

The piece has a romantic spirit. Shelley's "Mont Blanc" comes to mind, as well as Blake's *Songs of Experience*, "Little Boy Lost" in particular, in which a little boy is "lost" because he has questioned the authority of the church. In "Glacier Tale," the chains of our condition are language itself, the presumptions and values coded into its structure our cage ("The preconditions for speech have already been set") which is demolished, quite interestingly, by the "gong in subjectivity that shatters preconditions, that transforms subjectivity."

Which is a profoundly romantic view.

Reference is made to Schopenhauer, "The world is will and idea," who was among the first of western, 19th century philosophers to contend that the universe is not a rational place. Schopenhauer has a special appeal for those who wonder about life's meaning. I'm not sure Schopenhauer would be of much comfort if I was lost on a mountain glacier, but the allusion deepens the import of this particular adventure, in which the vagaries of human consciousness assume center stage: "Ceaselessly interrogating the real the mind is lined with feelings the way a beaver is with fur, a frigate bird with feathers."

Do the kids get down? Are they found? Suffice it to say the ice is musical, imbued with an immanence of the divine: ""During the night I could hear the ice hum,' the girl says to her brother. 'Did you hear it, John? Will we find our way down? I want to hum the music for Father.'"

The heart of this work is the sublime, especially Schopenhauer's conception of the sublime, which is a feeling of the beautiful so intense that it invites the observer to transcend individuality, but equally so threatening in its magnitude or vastness that prolonged exposure could destroy the observer.

Mountains are natural repositories of the sublime. The rock, the ice, the elevation, the caprices of wind and storm, the sheer massive thrust of the thing is a zone of stratospheric awareness, yanking us out of our complacency. "It makes no attempt to sound human," observed the Italian photographer and mountaineer Fosco Maraini with reference to Pakistan's K2. "It makes no attempt to sound human. It is atoms and stars. It has the nakedness of the world before the first man – or of the cindered planet after the last."

Zhang Er's *First Mountain*: Marriage and the "Incommensurable"

☆

David Karp

Zhang Er's *First Mountain* comes from a great distance, after a fair bit of time and over a much greater, epochal chasm: the over 2000 years that have passed since the Book of Rites, one of the Five Chinese Classics, was codified; and the over 100 years of Chinese Westernization and modernization that saw the Chinese state make efforts to erase the culture of which that Book was one expression. To put it as the book does, the poems are "souvenirs of space travel, / tickets for an underground train./ Even the seats/ are in flames." The original, Chinese-language book was inspired by a family obligation: the poet's 2001 participation in her family's reburial of the ashes of her grandmother and grandfather near their ancestral village in Shanxi province, China. During the ritual process that preceded, included and followed the reburial, the poet discovered, as she told Paul Nelson in an interview, "a gaping hole in my life—" the gape of her place in her own family and of its history because of her secular Communist upbringing, her globalized, metropolitan subjectivity and the simple fact that she had never visited this rural outpost of China. To find what was concealed in that "gaping hole," she took notes, then researched rites, customs regional and family history for several years. In 2004 she published the resulting poems as *Shan Yuan*, which translates as "first mountain," but also as "mountain source"; she considers the poems in it to be explorations of her core identity that provide not so much meaningful revelations as urgent queries and questions: "the whole book is a process of self-questioning."

It was not until 2008 that she began to collaborate with Joseph Donahue on transcribing the density of the Chinese-language poems into English that spreads out and elucidates what the Chinese language magisterially coalesces. It was another seven years before Donahue and Zhang Er finished turning these initial transcriptions into deft English poetry. Donahue has filled the short enjambed lines that dance all over the page with a glancing, allusive language. His words allow English-language readers to engage Zhang Er's questions and discover, at least provisionally, what she has answered. Since her questions are about basic human meaning-making activities—love-making, family-making, death-dealing, poem-writing itself—the answers matter. But they aren't always reassuring.

The book begins with a "Prelude" which establishes recurring themes and motifs. The entire ritual journey to honor her grandparent is imagined on the very first page as an embroidered landscape, the kind made for centuries precisely for such mental journeys:

> Turn on a light.
>
> > Illumine my dream
> > with more than just bright
> >
> > > > anticipation...
> > > a road branches
> > >
> > > > > > a window....
> >
> > > mountains hang on the wall
> > > > maddening, meticulous
> > > Every tree, a bright thread,
> > > every fold, pure silk
> > > pinch of fingers,
> > >
> > > > > > a needle
> > >
> > > nonetheless we arrive
> > > sky-high village, centuries old.

The journey, then, and the marriage it memorializes, are seen as part of a pattern created over time and through generations of family history. What is notable here is not only the connection of the journey to artistic process, but the tactile quality of this dream. Throughout the book, whatever is being evoked, celebrated, or interrogated, the flesh and its love-child desire will be asked to bear witness as well. At almost every point, whether the ostensible subject is family or ritual, the poet will also insist upon both the reality of the body and its needs, often humorously, often in a ravishingly sensuous way. She will also insist on the fact that the senses and the body vanish. Questions about the relationship of family history, marriage and parenthood, emerge alongside questions about the meaning of love, sex and longing; and all of those are pitted against death and time, which challenge their substantiality.

This essay considers the questions this book asks about human relationships and about marriage in particular, and the answers or the lack thereof embodied in the poems. In simplest terms, they are: What makes a marriage meaningful? What does a marriage amount to in the face of waning and wayward desire and, beyond all that, in the face of the immensity beyond our human lives? There are many other avenues to pursue in this book: the changes rung on the motifs of fire and water; the poet's dual embrace and questioning of her family history and of traditional rituals; her working out of several kinds of grief in the face of death and loss; the arguments about poetics that run throughout the book; the poet's mercurial ability to move between impassioned lyricism and brusque irony. However, this question of marriage and its ultimate significance is more than enough to tackle, and certainly essential to Zhang Er's vision; the book makes it clear that the questions she asks about marriage are difficult, maybe even intractable, but that they demand a response.

****

At the beginning of the book, in the "Prelude," the poet ponders her grandparents' seventy-year marriage:

"Watch them, the man and woman.

Each takes the end of a strip of red satin.

A marriage ritual.

>Walking down the slope,

>>walking up the slope.

This stark, archetypal image of married life as a walking up and down a mountain together is one the book returns to repeatedly. It is a powerful shorthand for their marriage, one that evokes stability and elemental timelessness but belies the marriage's social, gendered complexity and personal mystery. The image seems to fit into the embroidery. As the poet explores her grandparents' world and meditates on her memories of it, she will touch on the complexities that came with modern Chinese history and social and gender hierarchy. But they are not her sole concern. When she participates in the rites and records of family life and death—the sweeping out of the tomb; the reciting of the record of the past and present generations, which she insists must now include women as well as men; the setting up of the spirit tent; the presentation of paper offerings, the gaudy, wayward procession from the tomb meant both to honor the dead and block their path back to the living—she comes to imagine, interpret and inhabit a place inside the embroidered picture: a place inside her rooted clan. Her senses reshape themselves to fit the new realities she considers. Arriving at "My Grandmother's Village" and at her grandmother's "first home," she responds to "the photos of ancestors on the wall":

A desire to trace the cheek bones with a finger

to cup with both hands

the curves of the chin, a petite nose

round moist lips,

to feel the glow of health,

the beauty of a daughter,

As I might feel the clear stream of the Apricot River.

Her grandmother's house allows the poet to imagine herself inside family history still present and tangible, history with a skin to touch and explore, herself akin to an ancestral matriarch. When she meets a modern representative of family matriarchy, "The Wife of my Elder Cousin," she notes her bluntness, her pride in her daughter, her strong-boned body marked by a neck-chuff, the only sign of weakness in this woman. But she addresses her most intimate words to the woman's daughter, an undeniably modern teenager who somehow brings her grandmother to radiant literary life:

> Her casualness conjures up
>
> ghosts on the tip of
>
> the brow of sunlight—
>
>
> I see you. Everywhere is you,
>
>   clear bright golden light
>
>   Shining in all directions.

(Note the trope of sunlight here. As we will see later in this essay, it is less affirmative than it seems.)

For all her celebration of her grandparents' memory and marriage, the question of what that marriage ultimately amounted to persists. The down-to-earth reality of her grandparents' long coexistence described in "Warm the Tomb" produces both remembrance and doubt:

> *Marriage*, you said, *it's all up to you.*
>
> The way you put it
>
>
> Grandma
>
> made it sound
>
>
> like fate, like the stars.
>
>
> The story of your lives
>
>   Is quite fuzzy in places,
>
>   *
>
> But the end is all too clear.

In the final poem devoted to the grandparents' reburial, "Seal the Tomb," the long life of the marriage becomes a series of conjectures:

> A marriage of seventy years,
>
> dare we say it was passionate?
>
> Or was it only these ashes
>
> in my cupped hand,
>
> no longer divisible.
>
> I bury you, you bury me.
>
> Lie down, I am here.
>
> I am here—
>
> As a sailor might say,
>
> our relationship was over
>
> the minute you left that hotel room.
>
> As the Buddha might say,
>
>   there is no room,
>
>   and there is no you.
>
> And since there is no you,
>
> I bury myself.
>
> Yellow
>
>   dirt covering
>
>   yellow
>
>   dirt…

Grief and personal longing are salient here, evoking a soul and body desiring its mate, but so is the irony that however long this marriage "was," in an earthly sense it is "over," in any physical sense substantially "dirt", and in any subjective or intersubjective sense "not." In the last analysis, the remembrance and mourning offered her grandparents are "in your name, for death's sake/ under death's name," and the poet still asks if they are not just "a few last/ mementos of a senseless/ and inexplicable world?" The poem ends by imagining the consciousness of the dead in a way that is riddled with a doubt and paradox that are only resolved by a familiar American poetic whatsit:

> You smell nothing,
>
> therefore you believe.
>
> [...]
> You don't believe,
>
> > therefore you see
>
> a sacred scarab.
>
> And over there,
> A red wheelbarrow.

William Carlos Williams' image here plays the a role like that, earlier, played by the fox-fairy Zhang Er's grandmother told her about as a child, which she imagines "Perhaps/ [...] lights the eternal light/ for you, illumines the road/ of your departure." In both cases, what is imagined is provisional yet essential, providing something concrete to ponder on if not exactly believe.

What does "Seal the Tomb"'s simultaneous celebration of the importance of her grandparents' marriage and questioning of that marriage signify? Early in the book, the speaker meditates on the stars she sees in night sky: "What we most admire are,/ for the most part, these/ erratic rays of light// from the incommensurate afar". In a sense, this whole book is Zhang's exploration of the way humans, who do not and cannot live in the "incommensurate," however sublime they may find it, mediate the various "incommensurate" realties that plague humanity—absence and distance, desire and its frustration, domesticity and infidelity, daily bodily persistence and the disasters that punctuate and threaten it, and the ultimate unmeasurable, death. Her grandparents' enduring marriage, the family history of which it is part, the rituals that shape its human significance, if not its ultimate one, and her own poetic exploration of its meanings, are all versions of that mediation. She is honest about why each has meaning but also about the limits of that meaning.

*****

Just as important as the poet's account of her grandparents' union is her placing a record of metropolitan domesticity, love, longing and lust next to that account. The private, fragile yet persistent, if not faithful, domestic and erotic history is the focus of the section entitled "Round the Tomb: Return on the Third." The title refers to the Chinese custom of returning to the tomb on the third day after burial to perfect the tomb's circumference and make further offerings to help the dead on their journey to their afterlife. In this section, there is a circling around a not-quite-dead past, but nothing is laid to rest or perfected. The poet dramatizes a modern story of domesticity disturbed by routine, time, desire and also intimations of the incommensurate realities that make life and love seem very slight.

Early in this section, the poet conjures an image of intimacy that is both evocative and evanescent, as if at any moment it could be overtaxed by the "incommensurate." "Winter Solstice" is a hymn to a moment of domestic delight, "a present for me--/ that can't be held." In the same poem, at peace and play with her daughter, the poet also zeroes in on her daughter's nursery-rhyme words: "Ashes, ashes,/ we all fall down!" "New Year's Resolution" is another captured moment of domestic felicity, evoking laughter, smiles, sunlight, "dreamy winter," but finally emphasizing the moment's fragility: "row,/ row, row,// gently…gently…" Poems like these elevate contented moments into artistic permanence, but the rowing in Zhang Er's poems is nothing like the archetypal Elizabethan rowing in a T.S. Eliot performance: it's not Symbolic, a call to what's past and what lasts. These are poems of delight in what disappears.

The section also forcefully doubts the final import of "walking up the mountain," directly challenging union with glimpses of a vast and empty after and around. "Gold" is a poem in which the speaker ravishingly finds, loses, dreams about and doubts moments of mutual satisfaction in the shifting glint of golden sunlight. The poem presents all those collected moments as gold, but gold in the same way as sunlight is golden: beautiful, enlivening but precious because also insubstantial and fleeting. Other poems suggest that the only place to preserve such moments and the feelings that pervade them is in poetry, what in the "Prelude" she calls "those scratch[es] on a page." And as for the persistence of connubial and romantic feelings?

Who really knows what

floods me or you, what details,

what meticulous

pornography.

Much of "Round the Tomb" is taken up with a suite of poems
dealing with infidelity, inconstancy, the phantasms of desire and its
waxing and waning, the need to let go of what is lost and the inability
to do so. Fire and burning repeatedly figure as imagery. When the
section's concluding poem, "Return on the Third Day," reintroduces
the extended family figures and ritual acts that run through the
rest of the book, the speaker wavers between proclaiming the
actions needful for mourning—"Show respect three times,/ turn
around, burn paper again"—and floundering over their efficacy:
"Mountain god, earth god,/ Do we bow to all four directions?/ Do
we repeat one, repeat two, repeat three/ hundred thousand of/
times reincarnations?/ Who presides here?" Ultimately, the section
concludes with an overture to persistent desire, one both mordantly
down-to-earth and vulnerable:

I am making peace

with myself, catching my breath

after masturbating

to a photograph

voice…nudity…you

melting.

My hand smells like wet dog.

the scent of sunrise,

shall I ask you?

If this poem, and all the poems in "Return to the Tomb on the Third
Day," remain committed to the idea of marriage, of living with and
loving another, that faith is only provisional, placed in the artifact the
poem creates to explore what's as much absurd, painful and fleeting
as it is essential.

So we are left with the long-lived, loved, impressive but

opaque world of the grandparents' marriage alongside this more pungent, plangent world bedeviled by desire and ephemera. How can the two be reconciled? The final section of the book, "Wu Tai Mountains," makes the attempt. It dramatizes a train journey out to a Buddhist pilgrimage site, but it is as if the travelers move but the journey never begins: "Has time even passed?/ Is this the same platform?/ or one just like it?/ The train is not departing/ tormenting". The last three poems of the book, do, however, arrive somewhere. "Secret Words" suggests in a debate with her partner that they must remake imagination under the sway of sutras and ritual discipline, less prey to the predations of desire. "The Death of Fifth Uncle" wrenchingly mourns the accidental death of a cherished symbol of old ways, finding less consolation in dharma and ritual but calling on the poet and reader to to protect and bless his spirit and set aside the "none" that flesh becomes. Finally, "Turkey Seeds" sets a table among family and friends, gluttonously, tenaciously alive, where "The oil is hot, the fire is bright,/ into the pot it all goes./ We sate and stew/ ourselves/ in this world/ pi-pi-pa-pa." The meal and song are ironic, disgusting, alluring, reassuring. We're all cooked and we still gather. There is a kind of compassion here, and no abjuring of the world.

Joseph Donahue has compared Zhang Er's vision to that of Emily Dickinson, commenting on how the Chinese poet understands Dickinson's "zero at the bone," the cold terror one feels in the face of oblivion. Zhang Er is also like Dickinson in that she does not rest in any one conviction. In this book, *First Mountain*, she honors and mourns her ancestors, explores the vicissitudes of family and history, fully registers loves' fire and furor, acknowledges both the vastness of eternity and the emptiness of desire, but—something Dickinson was too intransigent to do—ends in sticky human stew. That seems about right for this deeply human book.

Rae Armantrout, *Wobble*

☆

Ken Cathers

Maybe with her there is always a "wobble"' at the center of things. Never quite clear if it is a seismic tremor or some interior event, a petit mal perhaps or some neurological quiver. Uncertainty always. There is a kind of temerity to her writing, a reticence, a reluctance to make the ephemeral real. Always this dance with the language, the reader; an austere courtship. What she almost says, steps back from, reconsiders, moves on to some unrelated thing she somehow connects becomes the way she insinuates herself into your favor.

There is a kind of algebraic logic to some of her poems. They are equations of words missing several steps, or too few variables, or solutions mysteriously arrived at. All this belied by a language hard, concise and tactile. Hers is a poetry of idea and image more than music. Often the poems are constructs of fragments, bits of line assembled into a semblance of meaning, an implied sanity to the order of things. She leaves questions unanswered, tensions unresolved. A subtle invitation to participate with or complete. One is always aware of a certain tone of wry irony that ranges from the skeptical to the devious. Best Proceed with Caution.

One feels the lack of passion or compassion in her writing. There is a cool, lunar austerity that calls to the senses rather than the emotions.. The poems are stripped down, connective tissue gone. There is more of what isn't than what is in her line; narrative, music, context minimalized. She invokes a willingness to hand over the controls to "the machine /that was language and feel what it wanted. . .steering only occasionally". ("The Craft Talk") Again, one wonders if this is something she really believes or something she just allows the poem to say. Caveat Emptor.

There is an attractive, tentative sense to her writing. At times one senses she is feeling her way into the dark or perhaps into the white silence of the blank page

> the contrived
> water bodies
>
> of say, peaches
>
> were just what you"d come
> to expect.
>
> was the first bit
> too cutesy?

Other times she seems to be annotating an unseen text or responding to statements we are not privy to

> Or what if
> pain
> and only pain
> can be
> alone?

Sometimes these play out like overheard snippets of gossip, one-sided phone conversations. This is her assent or rebuttal or contempt for whatever it is she responds to. But not a dialogue. These are her thoughts from the inside, the very process of ideation. So much of the groundwork has already been done. She does not have to explain. She is able to knit links together, make leaps into the ether because she has lain a framework beforehand.

Sometimes, if you listen carefully, a little is enough.

Notes on Contributors

Rae Armantrout's most recent books, *Versed, Money Shot, Just Saying, Itself, Partly: New and Selected Poems, Entanglements*, (a chapbook selection of poems in conversation with physics), and *Wobble* were published by Wesleyan University Press. *Wobble*, a finalist for the 2018 National Book Award, was selected by *Library Journal* as one of the best poetry books of 2018. In 2010 her book *Versed* won the Pulitzer Prize in Poetry and The National Book Critics Circle Award. In 2007 Armantrout received a fellowship from the Guggenheim Foundation. Her poems have appeared in many anthologies and journals including *Poetry, Conjunctions, Lana Turner, The Nation, The New Yorker, Bomb, Harper's,The Paris Review, Postmodern American Poetry: a Norton Anthology, The Open Door: 100 Poems, 100 Years of Poetry Magazine*, etc. She is recently retired from UC San Diego where she was professor of poetry and poetics. She lives in the Seattle area.

Stephen Bett is a widely and internationally published Canadian poet with 24 books in print. His personal papers are archived in the "Contemporary Literature Collection" at Simon Fraser University. His website is stephenbett.com

Ian Brinton's recent publications include a *Selected Poems & Prose of John Riley* and *For the Future, a festschrift for J.H. Prynne* (both from Shearsman Books), a translation of selected poems by Philippe Jaccottet (Oystercatcher Press) and he is working on an autobiographical account of Teaching English. His translations from Mallarmé with Michael Grant was just published by Muscaliet. He co-edits *Tears in the Fence* and *SNOW* and is involved with the Modern Poetry Archive at the University of Cambridge.

Ken Cathers has a M.A. from York University in Toronto. He has been published in numerous periodicals and anthologies. He has published 6 books of poetry and has a seventh book forthcoming from Ekstasis Press next year. He lives on Vancouver Island and is married with two sons and three grandchildren.

Karen Emmerich is a translator of Greek poetry and prose, and an Associate Professor at Princeton University.

Norman Fischer is a poet, essayist, and Zen Buddhist priest. His latest poetry titles are the serial poems *Untitled Series: Life As It Is* (Talisman House) and *On a Train At Night* (Presse Universite de Rouen et Havre). His latest prose work is *The World Could Be Otherwise: Imagination and the Bodhisattva Path* (Shambhala). He lives in Muir Beach, on the California coast.

Nancy Gaffield is the author of five poetry publications, most recently *Meridian* (Longbarrow Press 2019). She adapted her first book of poems, *Tokaido Road* (CB editions 2011) into a libretto; the opera, composed by Nicola LeFanu, premiered at the Cheltenham Music Festival in 2014, which toured nationally 2014-15. Her recent work, *Weald[en]* explores the consonance between nature, poetry and electronic music. She is a Reader in Creative Writing at the University of Kent.

Peter Hughes, currently based in north Wales, is a poet and the founding editor of Oystercatcher Press. He has written eccentric versions of Petrarch, Cavalcanti and Leopardi. His most recent book, *A Berlin Entrainment*, is published by Shearsman.

David Karp has lived in Seattle, Washington for over thirty years, and has taught English and Art History at Holy Names Academy for over twenty of those. He is associated with the Belltown poetry reading series Margin Shift, curated by the writers Matt Trease and Deborah Woodard. Among his fondest literary memories are sitting in on a University of Washington luncheon with Thom Gunn; hearing Peter Culley read for the last time in Seattle; watching Tongo Eissen-Martin's incendiary performances; and listening to both Zhang Er and Joe Donahue read at Margin Shift.

Recent books by **Robert Kelly:** *Seaspel, a pilgrimage*, Lunar Chandelier. *Ten Fairy Tales*, McPherson. Forthcoming: *The Work of the Heart*, an experimental novel. *The Cup*, a long poem. I teach in the Written Arts Program at Bard College. Met George Economou in graduate school at Columbia in 1956, and with him founded and edited *Trobar*, a magazine of the new American poetry.

Kevin Killian's poetry collections include *Argento Series* (2001), *Action Kylie* (2008), *Tweaky Village* (2014), which Macgregor Card chose for a Wonder Prize, and *Tony Greene Era* (2016). Killian's poems were anthologized in *Best American Poetry* (1988, edited by John Ashbery) and *Discontents: New Queer Writers* (1992, edited by Dennis Cooper). He was also the author of *Selected Amazon Reviews* (2006); the novels *Shy* (1989), *Arctic Summer* (1997), and *Spreadeagle* (2012); the short-story collections *Little Men* (1996), which won the PEN Oakland award; *I Cry Like a Baby* (2001), and Lambda Literary Award-winner *Impossible Princess* (2009); and the memoir *Bedrooms Have Windows* (1989).

Killian contributed significantly to scholarship on the life and work of American poet Jack Spicer. With Lewis Ellingham, he coedited Spicer's posthumously published detective novels *The Train of Thought: (Chapter III of a Detective Novel)* (1994) and *The Tower of Babel* (1994) and cowrote the biography *Poet Be Like God: Jack Spicer and the San Francisco Renaissance* (1998). With Peter Gizzi, Killian coedited *My Vocabulary Did This to Me: The Collected Poetry of Jack Spicer* (2008), which won the American Book Award from the Before Columbus Foundation.

He was the author of more than 30 plays for the San Francisco Poets Theater, including *Stone Marmalade* (1996, with Leslie

Scalapino), *The American Objectivists* (2001, with Brian Kim Stefans), and *Often* (2001, with Barbara Guest). With David Brazil, he edited *The Kenning Anthology of Poets Theater: 1945–1985* (2010). Killian's *Stage Fright, Plays from the San Francisco Poets Theater* appeared this year.

With his wife Dodie Bellamy, Killian edited the literary and art journal *Mirage #4/Period(ical)* and the anthology *Writers Who Love Too Much: New Narrative Writing, 1977–1997* (2017). He taught at California College of the Arts and lived in San Francisco before his death in 2019.

Stacey Levine's books include *The Girl with Brown Fur: Tales and Stories, Frances Johnson* (a novel), *Dra---* (a novel), and *My Horse: And Other Stories*. A recipient of a PEN/West Fiction award and a Stranger Genius award for literature, her work has also appeared in *The Fanzine, The Iowa Review, Quarterly West, Tin House (RIP), LIT, Yeti, Bookforum*, and other venues. Her novel *Where Is Mice?* will be published in 2020.

Susan McCaslin is a Canadian poet from Fort Langley, British Columbia who has published fifteen volumes of poetry, including her most recent, *Into the Open: Poems New and Selected* (Inanna, 2017). She has recently collaborated with J.S. Porter on a volume of creative non-fiction, *Superabundantly Alive: Thomas Merton's Dance with the Feminine* (Wood Lake, 2018). Her *Demeter Goes Skydiving* (University of Alberta Press, 2012) was shortlisted for the BC Book Prize for Poetry (Dorothy Livesay Award) and the first-place winner of the Alberta Book Publishing Award (Robert Kroetsch Poetry Book Award) in 2012. That year, she initiated The Han Shan Poetry Project in a successful effort to help save a rainforest near her home along the Fraser River outside Fort Langley, BC. Susan can be found wandering along the Fraser outside Fort Langley, BC with her dog Rosie in the presence of Douglas firs, hemlocks, and cedars. www.susanmccaslin.ca

Rick Moody is the author of six novels, three collections of stories, and three works of non-fiction, most recently the memoir *The Long Accomplishment* (Henry Holt). He writes regularly about music at *The Rumpus*, and has an occasional column at *LitHub*, "Rick Moody, Life

Coach." He teaches at Brown University.

Glenn Mott is author of *Analects on a Chinese Screen*, a book of poetry set against China's rise to globalization. His *Eclogues on a Mustard Seed Garden* will be published by Turtle Point Press in Fall 2020. He is publisher of Polymorph Editions, a press focused on translations of Asian writers, which will publish *No Poetry: The Selected Poems of Che Qianzi* in Fall 2019.

John Olson has published numerous books of poetry and prose poetry, including *Dada Budapest, Larynx Galanxy,* and *Backscatter: New and Selected Poems.* He has also published four novels: *In Advance of the Broken Justy, The Seeing Machine, The Nothing That Is,* and *Souls of Wind.* His essays have appeared in numerous publications, including *The American Scholar, KYSO Flash* and *Writing On Air.*

Toby Olson's just-published poetry book is *Death Sentences* (Shearsman). His eleventh novel, *Walking,* will appear at year's end from Chatwin Press.

Rochelle Owens, a central figure in the international avant-garde is a poet,playwright, translator, editor and video artist. The author of four collections of plays and eighteen books of poetry, including recently *Hermaphropoetics, Drifting Geometries* (Singing Horse Press) and *Out of Ur-- New and Selected Poems* (Shearsman), other poetry collections are *Solitary Workwoman* and *Luca, Discourse on Life and Death* (Junction Press). She is a recipient of five Village Voice Obie awards and Honors from the New York Drama Critics Circle and is widely known as one of the most innovative and controversial writers of this century whose groundbreaking work has influenced subsequent experimental poets and playwrights. Since its first publication in 1961, her play *Futz* has become a classic of the American avant-garde theatre and an International success. Her work has been translated into Danish, French, German, Greek, Italian, Japanese, Swedish and Ukrainian.

Marjorie Perloff is the author or editor of many books on twentieth and twenty-first century poetry and poetics, including *The Poetics* *of Indeterminacy: Rimbaud to Cage* (1981), *The Futurist Moment: Avant-Garde, Avant-Guerre, and the Language of Rupture* (1986), *Wittgenstein's Ladder* (1996), and *Unoriginal Genius* (2014). The University of New Mexico Press has just published a two-volume selection of her book reviews from 1969 to 2019, which includes reviews of figures as varied as Harold Bloom and Laurie Anderson, and of translations from Hölderlin to Haroldo de Campos. She is the Sadie D. Patek Professor of Humanities Emerita at Stanford University.

Ron Silliman's projects for 2019 include *Five Poems I Did Not Write* and *Season of the Which*, two chaplets from Happy Monks Press, *The L=A=N=G=U=A=G=E Letters: Selected 1970s Correspondence between Bruce Andrews, Charles Bernstein and Ron Silliman*, edited by Matthew Hofer & Michael Golston, from the University of New Mexico Press, and *Il Quaderno Cinese / The Chinese Notebook*, a bilingual edition translated into Italian by Massimiliano Manganelli, from Tiellici Editrice: Benway Series. Forthcoming is an expanded edition of *Legend*, co-authored by Andrews, Bernstein, Steve McCaffery and the late Ray di Palma, also from the University of New Mexico Press. He lives near Valley Forge, Pennsylvania.

Brian Smale: A native of Canada, he's widely known for his portraits of the world's leading businessmen and women, scientists, inventors, politicians, and a few very interesting oddballs. His work has appeared in *Fortune, Business Week, Forbes, Fast Company, Esquire, GQ, Rolling Stone, Communication Arts, American Photography, Texas Monthly* and *Spin*. Brian resides in Seattle with his wife, two goofy kids, and the the sloth-like dogs Mabel and Banksy.

Anne Tardos, a translingual poet, is the author of ten books of poetry and several performance works. Her writing is renowned for its fluid use of multiple languages and its innovative forms. Recent books of poetry include *The Camel's Pedestal, NINE,* and *I Am You*. She is the editor of three posthumous volumes of poetry by Jackson Mac Low. *The Writer,* a new volume of her poems is forthcoming from BlazeVOX in 2020. Fellow in Poetry from the New York Foundation for the Arts, Tardos lives in New York.

Esther Yi was born in Los Angeles in 1989. She is a writer living in Leipzig.

New books from grandIOTA

Fanny Howe
BRONTE WILDE

This early novel, briefly in print in the 1970s, has been revised by Fanny Howe and is now published in this form for the first time. It is also her first novel to be published in the UK. It is the tragic tale of a dispossessed young woman in thrall to a childhood friend, set against the background of the emerging counter-culture of the early 1960s. We love it and think it's up there with her best work.

JAN 2020 978-1-874400-75-2 158pp $13.50 (US) £10 (UK)

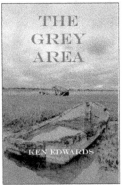

Ken Edwards
THE GREY AREA

A mystery novel in which the mystery seems incapable of any single solution. The action takes place in a mythical, contemporary English setting near the coast, and on the edge of a vast marsh. The detective is an illegal resident in a business park. His assistant is more concerned with her seven-year-old son who is failing at school. It's poetry by other means.
(An extract was published in *Golden Handcuffs* Vol II Issue 24.)

JAN 2020 978-1-874400-76-9 300pp $13.50 (US) £10 (UK)

grandIOTA *is dedicated to imaginative prose writing. We aim to publish books that are out of the ordinary, hard to categorise but good to read.*

You can order books from our website or from your favourite online or offline retailer. Please visit for up to date news and to go on the mailing list.

www.grandiota.co.uk

CPSIA information can be obtained
at www.ICGtesting.com
Printed in the USA
FSHW020603021119
63663FS